GATHERING STORM

A TANGLED HEARTS NOVEL

SARA CLARIDGE

Gathering Storm © 2015 by Sara Claridge

Paperback Edition

ISBN 978-2-9570785-4-7

CHAPTER 1

The torrential rain suited Jean-Luc's black mood. Between his bank informing him that yet again his sister's account was overdrawn and discovering that a shipment from China had been lost at sea, he'd had his work cut out that day.

He was nearly home when a warning triangle close to the curb made him reach for the hazard lights of his SUV. The heavy downpour had turned into a drizzle, and through the gloom a blue car with British plates appeared in the middle of the carriageway. Standing beside the Peugeot and looking extremely wet was the silhouette of a curvaceous woman.

Jean-Luc sighed in irritation. He didn't have time to rescue damsels in distress today. Not even ones with great legs.

When she raised a boot-clad foot and kicked the car's tyre with force, almost falling over backwards in the process, Jean-Luc couldn't help a reluctant smile. He'd wanted to hit something himself for most of the day and could sympathise with her frustration.

He pulled the car over behind hers and admired the view as she walked towards him. Hips swaying with each step, her T-shirt rose up to offer a tantalising glimpse of her midriff as she stuffed a phone into the pocket of her skirt. That explained some of her problem.

The signal would be patchy at best in the storm. Even his phone, boosted by the SUV's electronics, was always weak along this stretch of road. With nothing but endless fields, chestnut plantations, and a wide expanse of sky, mobile masts weren't a priority in this part of France.

As she approached his car, he slid the window down and raised his voice so she could hear him above the rain. "Bonjour, what appears to be the problem?"

She drew level with his door and leaned in. His breath caught as his gaze was captured by the most mesmerising green eyes he'd ever seen. Her grateful look almost made him feel guilty for his thoughts as his eyes followed the long strands of her wet hair downwards to where her rain-soaked top outlined her breasts to perfection.

Almost, but not quite.

"Thank you so much for stopping."

He expected the clear-cut British accent, but there was a softness to it and a hint of uncertainty in her eyes that countered any harshness in the tone. As she spoke, the musky scent of sweet chestnut trees in full flower drifted through the open window, assailing his nostrils and doing nothing to clear his mind.

She gestured towards the car, drawing his attention away from his wayward thoughts. "I have no idea what happened. One moment I was cruising along cursing my mother, and the next all the warning lights came on, and then nothing."

"Did she deserve it?"

A moment's confusion crossed her face. Then the reserve that had previously shielded her eyes was replaced by a sparkle. "Absolutely." Her tone brooked no argument, but a smile lit up her face and his groin tightened in response.

Another car approaching from the opposite direction reminded Jean-Luc of her predicament. The roads weren't narrow here, but her car was too far away from the verge to be abandoned when visibility was so poor. He glanced at the clock on the dashboard. He needed to get on, but he could spare five minutes to help push her vehicle out of harm's way.

"We should move your car over to the grass verge before someone hits it." Without waiting for her to respond, Jean-Luc reached for the door handle, and she stepped aside.

His shoes hit the tarmac, and muddy water splashed up the trousers of his suit, soaking through. He shut his eyes tight and sent up a silent apology. The sound of his house-keeper tutting when she saw the state of them was already ringing in his ears. It was like being eight years old all over again.

Rolling up the sleeves of his silk shirt, he considered the best option. "If I push and steer the car over, can you give a shove from behind?"

"Yes, of course." She walked round to the back of the vehicle.

Jean-Luc imperceptibly shook his head as he watched her wipe her hands on her skirt before placing them firmly on the rear of the car, testing its resistance, her expression deadly serious. Did she think she could make up in mental strength what she lacked physically to move a ton of metal? He couldn't decide if it was cute or delusional.

The truth was he probably didn't need her help, but he

didn't want to tell her now. She looked like she'd be as prickly as his sister if she thought he was making allowances for her because she was female.

He checked that the gear stick was in neutral before leaning against the jamb, pushing the car toward the verge, steering with his left hand. As it started to roll forward, he felt the assistance coming from behind. Perhaps he'd under-estimated her strength.

Jean-Luc turned to give a smile of thanks, and a wave of lust ran riot through his body at the sight of her gaping neckline. Muttering a curse as he almost lost his footing in the wet grass, he focused his attention back on steering the vehicle.

With the car safely off the road, Jean-Luc shut the door and remembered his manners as he swung around to face her.

"Sorry, I forgot to introduce myself. Jean-Luc Delacroix." He held out his hand.

"Madeleine Smythe." Despite the cool, clipped response, as her warm, slender fingers curled around his palm, his heart rate sped up. He hadn't imagined it. Those emerald eyes dazzled him.

"Enchanté, Madeleine," he said, appreciating the way her name slid off his tongue like melted butter.

"Thank you for your help. I didn't know what to do next." Her grateful tone possessed a hint of desperation. "I've been here almost twenty minutes and not one car has passed by." She reached into her pocket and held up her mobile. "And typically, just when you need this, it's totally useless—no signal. I debated whether I should start walking, but the rain..." She drifted off, holding out her hand, watching it for a moment as a lone raindrop bounced off her palm.

"It's a bad day for travelling, n'est-ce pas? Maybe you should have stayed at home."

Madeleine raised an eyebrow at him. Okay, perhaps it wasn't any of his business.

"Maybe I didn't have a choice. What's your excuse?"

He smiled. "Touché. But I grew up in this part of France and know the roads well, certainly better than a tourist."

Besides, he needed to get home tonight in case Chantal returned from her latest excursion. He worried when his sister was away from home, particularly after Danielle had said she'd been upset when she'd left for Paris. Not that either he or his housekeeper had heard from her since, except for a text.

A streak of lightning blazed down in the road ahead, followed by a loud crack of thunder that reverberated menacingly. Madeleine jumped towards him, visibly startled by what was probably a precursor to another downpour.

She was about five-six, a good deal shorter than his six-one, and completely soaked to her skin. Now that she stood closer, he could see the rivulets of water slide down her pale neck and beyond. Was it chivalry or desire that made him want to reach out and protect her from the rain?

"You don't have a waterproof coat?" Surely a raincoat was the one thing an Englishwoman would own.

A ghost of a smile crossed her lips. "I'm packed for the Caribbean."

Now it wasn't just his libido aroused, but his curiosity, too. "You were expecting a little more sunshine and a little less rain."

"Yes." She laughed shakily as another flash lit up the grey sky. "But I didn't expect so much rain here, either."

He shrugged. "It's a relief after the last two weeks. It's the hottest June on record. Are you staying locally?"

"I'm on my way to visit my mother in Bergerac, but I think I might have a taken a wrong turn."

Bergerac was still a couple of hours away even in good weather. Perhaps fate had done her a favour. In today's storm she'd be lucky if she arrived in one piece. Maybe for once fate had indulged him, too.

"You're on the right route, but it's still some distance."

She sighed and scanned up and down the road before turning her gaze back to him with hope in her eyes. It made him want to protect her and kiss her senseless at the same time.

When her tongue slipped out to remove a drop of water from her lips, he nearly groaned out loud. An icy raindrop landing on the back of his neck stopped him. Another one, heavier this time, landed on the back of his shirt and soaked through. The next storm was only minutes away, and whilst a cold shower might do him some good, they really needed to take shelter.

"I don't suppose there's a garage nearby that might be able to help me get the car started again?" Green eyes regarded him wistfully, and his resolve not to get involved melted away. Merde. She wouldn't like his reply.

"Not on a Saturday afternoon. This is a rural area. Every-where around here closes at midday."

"I thought you might say that." She spoke quietly, the hopeful expression on her face replaced with resignation. He reached out and gave her shoulder a brief squeeze of sympathy.

Before he gave it a second thought and allowed time for reason to take hold, he offered yet more assistance.

"You are welcome to come home with me. You can dry yourself and telephone your mother, let her know that you will be delayed."

She didn't respond verbally, but raised her eyebrows in a disdainful way that said she wasn't born yesterday. Jean-Luc was undeterred. Persuading people to bow to his command was one of his talents, at least some of the time. Although, after the way he'd been admiring her, perhaps she had a point.

He gave a soft laugh, acknowledging her unspoken candour. "Don't worry. We won't be alone. My housekeeper is there, and I promise to be on my best behaviour." Jean-Luc regarded the darkening sky and then looked back at her with what he hoped was an air of reassurance. "The next storm is about to hit us, and when it does, there will be no hope of either of us getting a mobile signal. From the house I can make some calls to see if someone is willing to come out and try to fix your car."

"I thought all the garages were closed?" The distrust was clear in her voice, and as she tilted her head to examine him more carefully, her eyes narrowed with suspicion.

She was wise to doubt him. After all, how would he feel if Chantal went off with a stranger? He went cold at the thought.

"They are, but in small communities everybody knows each other. Just because their business is closed, it doesn't mean I can't ring them at home to ask for a favour." He could sense a chink in her armour on the use of the word favour. It was as if she recognised he was putting himself out to help her. "Also, I think you need somewhere to change out of those clothes, before you are the one needing a warning triangle."

Her cheeks went bright pink as she glanced down at her top that no longer covered as much of her wet as it did dry.

Very smooth, Jean-Luc. Now she's definitely going to think you're only interested in one thing.

"Sorry. I didn't mean to say it as I did." He held her embarrassed gaze, regretting his stupidity. "I meant it when I said you will be safe with me, and I promise not alone."

What else he could say to persuade her? A tentative smile crept up on Madeleine's face, surprising him.

"If you're sure it wouldn't be too much trouble?"

Too much trouble? It was turning out to be the highlight of his day.

The thought had no sooner crossed his mind when the heavens opened and they made a dash for his car.

HOPING A PSYCHOPATH WASN'T LIKELY TO BE DRIVING A CAR that must have cost at least three times what she earned a year, Madeleine sank into the luxury of Jean-Luc's SUV.

In reality, it wasn't him Madeleine didn't trust. Instinct told her he'd keep to his word. It was her own reactions that concerned her. From the moment she'd leaned into the car window to speak to him, her skin had tingled with attraction. She couldn't make up her mind if it was the sexy French accent or his dark Gallic elegance that played havoc with her normally easy resistance to men. Dinner and a movie with a couple of the girls from work held more appeal than a night out spent trying to appease a male ego.

But for someone who could make the hair stand up on

the back of her neck with a heated glance, well, perhaps she'd reconsider, given the opportunity.

"Are you going to your mother's for a holiday?" Jean-Luc's deep voice broke into her thoughts.

"Something like that, though it's not normally relaxing enough to call a holiday." She grimaced inwardly. No, definitely not a holiday. Going to the Caribbean to stay with her friend Kathy was a vacation, but all hope of that vanished the instant she'd foolishly answered the phone two days ago. One day she'd take some time off that didn't involve some trauma with her mother, but it wasn't going to be this year.

She reached down to adjust her skirt. A dark stain spread across the leather seat as water poured off her and soaked into the upholstery.

"I should have fetched a towel out of my bag." Appalled at the damage she'd caused, Madeleine searched through her handbag looking for something suitable to mop up the remaining water before she ruined the interior, but even her packet of tissues were limp from the rain.

Jean-Luc gave her a puzzled stare.

"By the time I get out, it's going to look like you've driven through a river." She groaned. "And that can only mean I resemble a drowned rat."

He smiled at her, his dark eyes glinting with amusement, and her heart fluttered.

"I think we've already covered that a drowned rat isn't the image that springs to mind." His gaze swept over her, and she grew warm. "La naïade would be more appropriate."

Berating herself that she was as bad as her mother if she fell at the feet of the first handsome guy who came to her rescue, Madeleine grasped at the opportunity to change the conversation.

"What's that?"

"I suppose you would call it a water nymph or sprite. My mother had a fascination for Melusine, a naïade who married a mortal man. When we were children, she would always tell us about the various legends surrounding Melusine throughout Europe."

For a moment Madeleine could imagine the small boy, listening intently, his tousled black hair, tanned skin, and eyes so dark they would melt the heart of the sternest mother.

"Was the sprite French?"

"No, I think she originated from Eastern Europe, but the story in France is she married a man on the condition he couldn't see her one night a week."

"When presumably she turned into a mermaid."

"Actually, she had the tail of a serpent, not a fish."

"What happened?"

He glanced at her again. The smile replaced by mocking curiosity. "You do not think they lived happily ever after?"

"Not in my experience."

Dark eyebrows raised slightly, and in that one sexy expression, Madeleine forgot all about the boy and fully appreciated the man beside her. A shiver went down her spine. He adjusted the car's heating. She didn't tell him that her reaction had nothing to do with the cold.

"He did what no one should ever do. He listened to gossip." Jean-Luc spoke almost to himself. For a fraction of a second, Madeleine had the impression he spoke from experience, but after one glance at his impassive face and she decided she'd imagined it.

"Her husband was jealous, convinced she was having an affair. Instead of leaving her alone as she had asked, one night he hid and watched her bathe. It was the last time he saw her. Rumour has it she still haunts the tower at Lusignan, though I think the original castle has long since been destroyed."

"Who cursed her in the first place?"

"Her mother."

"Figures. I often think my mother's done the same to me."

He laughed, his deep tone reverberating inside the car. His smile was infectious, and Madeleine smiled back, pushing her worries about where they were headed to the back of her mind.

"She cannot be that bad. You are going to stay with her, after all?"

"Don't you believe it. I said I was on my way there, not the reason why." The upturn of her mouth softened the sharpness of her tone. "My mother always manages to turn my holidays into rescue missions from whichever desolate country she's living in."

"Not quite how they describe France in the tourist brochures." His sardonic tone nagged at her conscience, and words of contrition rushed to her lips. "Perhaps you don't appreciate how much your mother misses you."

She almost choked with indignation on her apology. Drop dead gorgeous or not, he'd just slid right down to lukewarm on the hot scale.

"Enough about mine. Does your mother still tell the story?"

"Not anymore." The inflection in his voice made Madeleine turn towards Jean-Luc. His jaw was tight and his gaze firmly on the road ahead. In a split second, he had become distant. "She died ten years ago."

Guilt flooded Madeleine. He didn't know what a nightmare her mother was. Perhaps having lost one was reason enough to defend someone else's.

"I'm sorry. I didn't mean to pry." Goosebumps spread out over her arms as the distance between them stretched further than the physical separation of the two front seats.

Jean-Luc changed the subject back to more neutral ground. "Don't worry about the car. It's had worse. It's one of the reasons I use it in bad weather. Anyway, the seats are leather, and they dry quickly."

Had he felt the loss of connection, too? "I thought the rain was exceptional—are you saying this is normal?"

"It can be, particularly at this time of year, but do not despair. The weather is supposed to clear this evening, and there will be blue skies for your holiday."

Ancient rooftops and turrets broke into the view of the valley beyond, a tall church spire at the centre. Before they reached the village nestled below the road, the car slowed, and Jean-Luc turned right. Awe filled Madeleine as they drove under an archway and past an enormous pair of gates, their intricate iron work weaving an abstract pattern that seemed to neither stop nor start at any particular point.

A long drive stretched ahead, flanked on either side by lime trees, their leaves swaying from heavily pollarded branches in the wake of the SUV. At the end of the private road stood a chateau, its round towers rising majestically into the stormy sky.

Jean-Luc pulled to a halt in front of the building. Austere, flat grey stone loomed over them, eerily lit by flashes of lightning. Despite the bad weather, or maybe because of it, the effect was like its inhabitant. Imposing, yet immensely entrancing.

"Wow!" Madeleine leaned forward and peered upwards through the windscreen. "Not what I expected. Have you lived here all your life?"

"Yes." At the proud note in Jean-Luc's voice, Madeleine turned her head towards him, only to find he was much closer than she thought. The scent of his aftershave mixed with the smell of summer rain had her senses running into overdrive.

"I forget sometimes how splendid it is when you see it for the first time." He spoke softly, his eyes darkening as his gaze captured hers, and suddenly Madeleine wasn't sure if he was talking about the chateau or her.

A wave of unexpected desire hit her. She could feel the warmth of his body as it radiated across from the driver's seat. The car's spacious interior became as cramped as her Peugeot. Her mouth went dry. Then heat surged into her cheeks. He'd seen her reaction.

Madeleine's breath caught in her throat. She broke eye contact and reached awkwardly for the door handle. "It's amazing. I can't wait to see it close up." Madeleine kept her gaze on the car door interior, knowing if she turned around she would see an amused tilt to Jean-Luc's mouth. She was running. He knew it. She knew it.

The sound of his mobile phone vibrating stopped her from making more of a fool of herself than she had already.

"Saved by the bell?" The slight challenge in his voice was all Madeleine needed to make a hasty escape.

CHAPTER 2

Certain she'd be safer inside the chateau than the confines of the car, Madeleine hurried up the flight of steps towards a huge oak door. It swung open as she approached, and a smartly dressed woman somewhere in her late fifties greeted her.

"Bonjour, madame."

"Hello, sorry... excusez-moi, bonjour." Still unnerved by her reaction to Jean-Luc, she took a deep breath to steady herself and stepped over the threshold.

Where the outside of the chateau was austere, the inside exuded luxury. Inlaid tile floors led the way to darkened corridors, and a magnificent stone staircase dominated one side of the hallway.

The woman, presumably the promised housekeeper, continued to regard her with an expectant look. Madeleine wracked her brains for a suitable French phrase, but her mind went blank with nerves. Jean-Luc came through the door and saved her from any further embarrassment.

The grey-haired woman turned her attention to him. She

dismissed Madeleine with a hasty glance as if to confirm she wouldn't understand the conversation, before talking to Jean-Luc in low undertones. Even if she could hear clearly, they spoke too fast for her to translate. However, from the few words she picked out using the French she'd learnt at school, Madeleine got the distinct impression it wasn't all about her.

Jean-Luc turned abruptly to her. An impenetrable mask replaced any previous warmth in his expression, though a rough hand through his hair gave away his frustration with the conversation.

"I missed a call from my sister." The implication being because he'd been helping her. He didn't need to say it. Madeleine saw it in his eyes.

"I'm sorry I delayed you. Is she okay?"

For a moment, a trace of conflict crossed his face. Did he want her to leave?

"I'm sure she's fine. I would like to telephone her to confirm it for myself." His voice gave nothing away. "After I've spoken to her, I'll call about your car."

This time he spoke to the housekeeper in English, and Madeleine groaned inwardly at her own ineptitude for misunderstanding the situation earlier.

"Danielle will show you to a guest room and find you some dry clothes to change into."

Madeleine opened her mouth to protest, but he held up his hand. "Please do not refuse. It's no trouble, and I do not want to be responsible for you catching a cold. I will be in the salon when you are refreshed." Without waiting for her response, he turned on his heel and walked through a narrow doorway to the left.

Slightly perturbed by the sudden change in atmosphere,

she chided herself for her lack of gratitude. Would she be as generous if the boot had been on the other foot? She suspected not. Giving what she hoped was a winning smile to Danielle's hesitant expression, Madeleine followed her up the staircase, admiring the paintings that hung on the walls.

As she closed the door to the bedroom she'd been shown to, she laid her forehead against the jamb and tried to collect her thoughts. They were clouded by images of a broad-shouldered, dark haired Frenchman instead, causing a warm sensation low in her body and a hardening of her nipples beneath her bra.

What was wrong with her? For someone who prided herself on never relying on a man for anything except sex, and not always for that, either, she'd turned into a gauche idiot in the car at the hint of something flirtatious. The confident financial analyst who could hold her own in a boardroom full of men had been washed away with the rain.

Not to mention that being attracted to the man who rescued her made her sound as flaky as her mother. Barbara Smythe might make it her business to always be on the lookout for a knight in shining armour, but after a lifetime of being the one who extracted her mother once she grew bored, Madeleine wasn't about to follow in her footsteps.

Exiling the images of the sexy Jean-Luc from her head, she turned around and admired the room. There was no doubt whoever had decorated this room had excellent, if not expensive, taste.

She wasn't sure what to expect when she'd agreed to come back with Jean-Luc, but the chateau had definitely been a surprise. She'd envisaged a bachelor pad, not an imposing manor house.

While the bedroom portrayed French, old-world charm with its panelled walls and enormous ornate bed, the bathroom was totally modern in stark contrast. She peeled the wet clothes away from her cool skin, turned on the shower, and stepped under the spray. The hot water felt glorious as it flowed over her, banishing the cold of the rain.

Madeleine reached for the shower gel and worked it into a lather over her body, enjoying the exotic scent of hibiscus rising in the steam. She closed her eyes for a moment, and her mind filled with thoughts of Jean-Luc. The way the cut of his shirt defined his biceps when he pushed her car. The heat emanating from his body when she stood next to him in the pouring rain.

The jets of hot water massaging her body did nothing to cool down her imagination.

Then a hardened edge came over the eyes of the enigmatic Frenchman and abruptly ended her day dream. Did his expression change before or after his conversation with the housekeeper?

Stepping out of the shower, Madeleine enveloped her body in a huge, soft bath towel and mentally shook herself for worrying about something that wasn't her concern. But a nagging voice still said there was more going on at the chateau than she understood.

As she walked back down the stairs a short while after, Madeleine wondered where Danielle had gotten the exquisite turquoise dress and cardigan that had been draped across the bed when she came out of the bathroom. With a house as grand as this, clothes were probably as much an accessory as the right champagne for the string of fashion-able women she imagined Jean-Luc entertained.

She paused for a moment at the bottom step and reached inwardly for the fortifying deportment she'd been taught at boarding school. Deep breath, spine straight, shoulders back, head up, tail in. Her mental armour back in place, she was ready to face the man who broke it down with just a look.

JEAN-LUC DIDN'T NEED TO GLANCE UP TO SENSE THE EXACT moment Madeleine entered the room. One minute he was seated in an armchair totally focused on the report in front of him, and the next his body was sending out alert signals. He looked over to where she stood and his mouth went dry. The dress she wore fitted like a glove, showing off her shapely figure to perfection as she hovered by the doorway.

"Thank you. I feel human again." A tentative smile formed on her lips.

Her dark hair fell in soft curls that swayed as she tipped her head. Green eyes that had already bewitched him continued to hold his gaze, though the confidence with which she'd entered the room seemed to be dissipating.

Where were his manners?

"Come in and take a seat. Did you find everything you needed?" He stood and walked towards her, placing the document he'd been studying on the coffee table. As he drew nearer, he realised his mistake. Close up, Madeleine had an even greater effect on his equilibrium as a hint of fresh fragrance infused the air, filling his mind with a vision of the shower she'd just taken. He already knew what she looked like wet with her clothes on. It wasn't hard for him to imagine her without them.

"The room was beautiful, and thank you for the loan." She held out the skirt of the dress.

"The colour suits you." Unable to resist the temptation, he reached out and toyed with the sleeve of the cardigan. He wondered if her skin underneath would be smooth like silk or sleek like satin to touch. Standing so close to her was intoxicating.

"I hope the owner doesn't mind me borrowing it."

Did he detect a note of curiosity in her voice? He held back a smile.

"Do not disturb yourself. I'm sure my sister will not object."

"Oh, did you manage to speak to her?"

"No. I left a message for her call." Chantal would ignore it, of course.

"Are you sure she won't mind about the dress? It might be new? It appears hardly worn."

"All her clothes have that appearance." Jean-Luc moved away from Madeleine back into the room. He needed to regain some clarity, and he couldn't do it standing next to her.

He'd been so wrapped up with work and Chantal that he hadn't been on a date in ages. Perhaps it was beginning to show. "I doubt she wears them all. Shopping is one of her favourite pastimes, and not only for clothes. Most of the rooms here feature something she's brought home from one of her excursions. The room you used was decorated by her."

"It's absolutely exquisite." Her obvious pleasure in the room lit up her face, and he felt a sense of pride in her appreciation of Chantal's expertise.

"Of course when I say decorated, I mean she chose the

colours and bought the furnishings—someone else did the hard work." It was a reprise of the friendly banter he and Chantal had shared many times.

She was the same age now as he'd been when he started the firm. But where he had drive and ambition, Chantal seemed content to drift through life, and it made him crazy. Then again, their life had been very different ten years ago, and she didn't have an eleven-year-old-sister to look after.

"The end result is really quite spectacular. She obviously has talent."

"But, as I'm always telling her, if she'd only apply her ability to earning, not just spending." The smile on his lips faded as he turned towards Madeleine, who still stood by the doorway. "However, I must remember to compliment her on her choice with this dress."

As the remark sank in, Madeleine's face turned a pretty shade of pink, and Jean-Luc restrained himself from closing the distance again. He needed to escape. He didn't need complications in his life, and Madeleine was definitely a complication.

"Take a seat and telephone your mother. I'll get us some coffee." He indicated the cordless handset on the table and made a hasty retreat.

He returned to the room as Madeleine hung up from her phone call. Placing the tray he carried on a table, Jean-Luc poured the coffee. "Did you speak to your mother?"

"Yes, everything is fine. I don't know why I expected it to be any different."

His gaze flickered to Madeleine's, and he frowned at her cryptic words. He'd been out of the room less than ten minutes, and yet he'd swear those beautiful green eyes that had examined him with a hint of hidden passion a few moments ago were now flashing with displeasure.

"You're right." Madeleine answered his unspoken question as she leaned forward to take the cup he offered her. "Everything is not fine." Her voice was sharp with annoyance. "Apparently my mother has taken it upon herself to arrange a trip for us down to the South of France with a friend, leaving this evening. Since I'm delayed, she's left a key for me with a neighbour."

"I take it you weren't expecting her to be going?"

Madeleine stood and walked over to the window, looking out at the expanse of garden beyond. From the rigid way she held herself, Jean-Luc could tell she was trying to figure out how much to tell him. He wanted to reach out to her, to offer comfort, but the anger radiating from every bone made him stay put, waiting for her to explain further.

"She does this to me every time, and no matter how often I tell myself I won't fall for it again, I do. You'd think after twenty-eight years I'd have learnt my lesson." Madeleine turned around to face him, her face marred with frustration. "I thought Manu National Park was bad, but this time she's excelled herself."

"You're not making any sense." He sipped his coffee, not wanting to turn her piercing gaze on him for the wrong reasons, though the fire burning in her was heating him up, too. What kind of sadist did it make him if he was turned on by her anger?

He let the Manu comment slide, filing it away for later. It would only confuse the point in hand if he asked her to explain. Every conversation with the confounding Madeleine Smythe seemed to leave him with more questions than answers.

She stared at him, bristling as if she expected him to understand more than he possibly could when they'd only just met.

"I drop everything to try and sort out her chaotic life, and what does she do? Scamper off at the first invite of someone wanting to cheer her up. I'm not sure who I'm mad at most. My mother for her ungratefulness or me for believing this time was different. I could kick myself."

"What made it different?" He softened his voice in an attempt to ease her tension. Madeleine took a deep breath and sighed, reigning in her emotions, taking the blaze he'd seen in her eyes down a notch as she calmed herself. It crossed his mind as to what it might take to put the spark back.

She took a couple of steps and leaned against a bookcase. "Normally my mother gets bored with her romances long before the current love of her life realises anything is amiss."

Jean-Luc smiled into his coffee cup. Cool, calm Miss British was back again, and he didn't know if he was disappointed or relieved as his heart rate slowed a fraction.

"This time it appears he wasn't so much interested in my mother's charms, more her money."

"Merde." The word slipped out before he thought to curb his language.

"Oh, don't you start lamenting over her misfortune." Her tone chastised him, but a wry smile revealed the comment was more sardonic than serious. "He's stolen a good portion, and I'm here to make sure he pays back every penny, but after four divorces my mother is far from broke. Besides, as this latest episode shows, it hasn't taken her long to find someone else to ride to the rescue."

"I take it the friend is male."

"I don't know any women named Gene."

"Gene Tierney."

"What?"

"Gene Tierney—you know, the American actress who played all those femme fatale roles such as Laura and Mrs Muir in The Ghost and Mrs Muir."

She raised an eyebrow.

"So my sister made me watch old movies." He shrugged.

Madeleine laughed, and Jean-Luc was pleased to see her body relax, the tension so visible on her face replaced by a smile.

"I'm pouring out my heart to you about my problems, and you start quoting black and white movies. I'm serious, you know. She drives me nuts."

"But I made you laugh." He crossed the room and lightly took her hand, pulling her to him. "Don't be so hard on yourself. It's difficult to say no to family."

He knew better than anyone. After their mother died, Jean-Luc had found it impossible to say no to Chantal, even though it was exactly what he needed to do. He put up boundaries such as her allowance to try and control her, but he also understood Chantal's reasons for constantly ignoring them.

"You don't have the monopoly on dysfunctional families, you know." He ran the back of his hand down her cheek, holding it there for a moment. "People think I'm the patient brother to my wayward sister, but the truth is she has me wrapped around her little finger. I've learnt not to come running, but it doesn't stop me bailing her out every time something goes wrong or caring when she has been hurt."

Madeleine's gaze swept up to meet his, and an array of emotions flickered through her eyes—from frustration to resignation with the situation. The vulnerability he saw there was his undoing. Jean-Luc lowered his head, no longer able to resist what he'd wanted to do from the moment he'd first caught sight of her a few hours ago.

His intention had been to comfort her and gently kiss her lips. But she tasted so good, so sweet, it was all he could do not to thrust his hands into her hair and pull her close to deepen the embrace.

He felt her tentatively return the pressure of his mouth against hers and savoured the softness of her lips. A sigh escaped her, and he took advantage of the depths they revealed to take the kiss further. Madeleine swayed closer, her mouth opening to his. Her hands spread out to explore his chest, and a wave of heat washed over his body. That was until he felt the slight push of resistance from her fingers.

The shrill sound of the phone made Madeleine leap back. She looked flushed and was breathing heavily, Jean-Luc noted with satisfaction, pleased that, like him, she was not unmoved by their encounter. Even if she had been about to put a stop to it.

"Saved by the bell again." His voice was laced with irony. "One of us has incredible luck with timing, no? I'm just not sure which of us it is."

He picked up the phone with a curt greeting. As he listened to the caller, Madeleine turned away to study the view through the window, putting some space between them and leaving him some privacy for the call.

Two minutes later he put the handset down. "That was the garage." She spun round, her eyebrows raised with anticipation, and his pride took a little fall that she seemed so eager to leave. "They couldn't get it started, so they towed it back to the workshop. They will try to fix it on Monday."

"See, that's what I mean." Annoyance was written all over her face again, the searing kiss pushed aside. "Mum is swanning around the south of France, while I'm left stranded in a country where I don't know anyone instead of relaxing in the Caribbean."

"Mais ma naïade." Jean-Luc kept his voice low. "You are not stranded, and you do know someone."

Madeleine turned towards him. "I'm sorry." She raised her hands in an apologetic gesture. "It wasn't very gracious of me. I sound like a petulant child, and you've been so kind."

For the second time that day, Jean-Luc found himself persuading her to trust him.

"D'accord—maybe you don't have a choice, but I'm hoping you'll stay. We can arrange for your bags to be collected, and tomorrow I can show you a little of this part of France." He laid his hand over his heart, giving her what he hoped was one of his most charming smiles. "And I promise to be on my best behaviour."

An impish glint appeared in her eyes, causing him to hold his breath for a fraction of a second, waiting for her answer.

"I'm sure you will. I'm just not sure whether your version of best behaviour fits in with mine."

CHAPTER 3

Had he forgotten about her? She'd been sitting in the salon for at least an hour and a half by herself, cooling her heels. After the garage had telephoned, the phone had rung again and Jean-Luc had intimated he'd take it elsewhere and might be some time. He raised his lips in silent apology, but that did little to mollify her after waiting alone for so long.

At the time she'd been secretly relieved to put some space between them. But now puzzlement, tinged with annoyance, crept to the fore on the thought that he'd abandoned her so easily, after kissing her so thoroughly.

Madeleine could still taste him on her lips, feel the strength in his body underneath her fingertips, and remember how his hands had burned a path as he held her securely in his embrace. It disconcerted her how willingly her treacherous body had begged for more. She was only thankful that somewhere in her head an alarm had gone off even before the phone had rung.

Falling at the feet of a guy after meeting him five minutes

before wasn't her style, no matter how devastatingly gorgeous he looked. It wasn't as if she was a stranger to handsome men. She'd been on plenty of dates with them, but something about Jean-Luc unsettled her.

Was it the wicked glint in his eyes when he smiled or the sensual curve of his lips that set off the tingling sensation she got every time he stood close? She should probably run while she had the chance, but giving in to the pleasure sure to follow was almost too tempting.

But it still didn't get away from the fact they were complete strangers. The salon, whilst beautifully furnished, held few clues to the person behind it. Madeleine would lay odds it had also been decorated by his sister, but the lack of family photos or memorabilia seemed strange in what was obviously a well-used room.

Even though her relationship with her mother was stormy, she still had a few pictures on display in her small London apartment of their lives over the years. However, this room was devoid of anything more personal than the occasional statue.

She couldn't even Google him. It would be worth the expense of data roaming, but her signal was still nonexistent, and she hadn't thought to ask about wifi access. The irony of asking Jean-Luc for a password so she could snoop on him brought a smile to her lips.

Rising out of the chair, Madeleine wandered about the room, pausing to study some of the titles on the books that lined the back wall. She had just reached for one of the volumes when the sound of his voice in the doorway made her spin round. Surprised, she stood her ground defensively. "Sorry, what did you say?"

All previous annoyances with him fled from her mind as

she took in the sight of Jean-Luc leaning against the door-frame. At some point he'd gone upstairs to change. The suit he'd worn had been replaced by a plain shirt and dark jeans that drew attention to his long, lean thighs. Damp hair curling around his collar had her thoughts wandering, picturing him in the shower, his naked body glistening under the spray.

"I asked if you were hungry."

The *yes* was almost a whisper on her lips before she realised it wasn't what he meant.

"It's nothing formal. Danielle normally leaves me some supper in the kitchen."

"Sounds perfect."

Pleased she'd managed to respond in a normal tone despite the hammering of her heart, Madeleine followed him down a passageway, dimly lit by the glow coming from the kitchen beyond. When she brushed past him as he held the door open for her, she decided being sensible was overrated. Surely she could learn enough about Jean-Luc over dinner to no longer consider him a stranger.

At Jean-Luc's suggestion she sat at the large oak table as he took a casserole dish from the oven. The aromas when he lifted the lid made Madeleine's stomach contract hungrily. She stamped down on her reaction, telling herself it was the thought of food that made her respond this way, not the view of his backside as he leaned down to the oven.

"I hope you don't mind eating in here." He turned around and caught her staring at him, making her blush furiously.

"No, not at all." She raised her hands in front of her to disguise her flaming cheeks, annoyed that this was becoming a habit around him.

"The dining room is rather grand. We only use it on formal occasions, so most of the time we eat in here. I prefer its intimacy."

Madeleine's heartbeat raced as eyes as dark as night stared directly at her, holding her gaze, their meaning clear. The cynical side of her silently asked how many intimate dinners he'd had here.

"I've been wondering what it would be like to grow up in an amazing place like this." She'd been thinking no such thing, but it was the first thing she thought of saying to try and put the conversation back on a more even keel. Whether Jean-Luc realised it, Madeleine wasn't sure, but he picked up her cue.

"As a boy I ran wild. I think I'm more than a bit responsible for Danielle's grey hair." His eyes crinkled as a wicked smile crossed his face. "There is so much space here and so many places to hide. My friend Raphael and I used to be constantly in trouble for one reason or another. However, I always made it home for lunch."

Madeleine found herself smiling back, picturing him once again as a young boy. "Danielle's cooking?"

"Oui." He shrugged. "That, and if you missed it, you went hungry for the rest of the day. Fortunately for me, now when she knows I haven't had time during the day to eat, dinner is a little more substantial."

The tempting aroma of boeuf bourguignon wafted up as Jean-Luc placed two plates in front of them and sat next to Madeleine at the head of the table. Ignoring the way her body responded to the nearness of him, she teased, "Ah, so she still looks after the little boy?"

He gave a disarming grin in reply and pointed with his

fork. "Eat. I guarantee it is the best home-cooked meal you will have ever tasted."

"Where I come from, that isn't saying much," she said, thinking of her typical microwave dinners for one, eaten hastily out of the carton in front of the TV most evenings. "Oh, this is fabulous! The meat simply melts in your mouth and the flavour, it's delicious."

"You don't eat at home often?" He poured them both a glass of red wine.

Madeleine took another mouthful of the casserole, trying to decide how lazy it would make her sound if she answered honestly. She gave a wry smile. "Let's just say I keep the convenience food industry in business. The last time I ate anything close to regular home-cooked meals was at boarding school—and believe me, it was nothing like this."

"You were sent away to school?" He sounded disapproving. She liked him all the more for it.

"My mother continually moved around. Boarding school meant she didn't have to worry about me for nine months of the year."

She didn't add that she'd rarely heard from her mother in between times. Weekend visits had been rare, and her mother had only brought her home during the holidays because there was nowhere else for her to go. Even then she was kept out of the way most of time, except, of course, for when it suited her mother to have a daughter.

Jean-Luc regarded her for a moment as if considering her reply. "What about your father?"

"I haven't seen him since I was about three. They divorced, he disappeared." She brushed it off as if it was nothing, but it had hurt that neither of her parents had wanted her around when she was growing up. Madeleine

took a sip of wine and diverted the conversation away from
her. "What about you? How come you got to torture
Danielle and not your parents?"

"They travelled a lot when I was very young, and I think
they thought it safer to leave me with Danielle until I was
older." Jean-Luc placed a morsel of beef in his mouth and
chewed it slowly. Madeleine waited, sensing he wanted to
say more. "But then my father died suddenly of a heart
attack. A little boy held few distractions for my mother, so
she absorbed herself by helping local artists."

A soft exclamation escaped her mouth in sorrow for the
child of the past.

"I didn't mind. I think I understood it was her way of
dealing with her grief. Danielle used to take care of the two
of us."

A nostalgic look came over him, and Madeleine knew
that, though they were both brought up by people who
weren't their parents, their childhoods were completely
different.

"What about your sister?"

"Chantal is my half-sister. Several years after my father
died, my mother married one of the artists she'd helped."
The shuttered expression she'd seen before came down over
his face as he stood. "Would you like some cheese?"

The subject was closed. Madeleine longed to probe more,
but she was hardly in a position to push when they'd only
just met.

In the accompanying lull in conversation, Jean-Luc
cleared their plates and laid out a selection of cheese. She
recognised some of the produce from regions she'd travelled
through earlier that day and reflected on the areas she'd
missed discovering on her journey down.

He broke the silence. "Why did you drive and not fly?"

Wow. Could he read minds? She hoped not. She'd also been admiring the way his muscles flexed under his shirt as he stretched up to reach for something from a cupboard above him.

"I've been asking myself that question ever since the rain started. The last time I came to France, I was a little girl. I thought since I was here using up my holiday allowance anyway I might as well see a little of the country, too."

"With your mother?" He sounded sceptical.

"No, definitely not. I presumed I'd finish up at a loose end, but I didn't think it would be this quick."

"Who was waiting for you in the Caribbean?" His voice was casual enough, but his pointed gaze asked a different question. Friend, boyfriend, lover? Apparently she wasn't the only one fishing for more information.

"An old friend from school. Though I suspect by the time I make it there, she'll have given up waiting. I don't suppose I'll manage the trip now until next year." She sighed wistfully as she thought about the ten luxurious days lying on a beach doing nothing more than figuring out which cocktail to drink next.

"I would say I'm sure your mother appreciates the sacrifice, but I have the impression you would not believe me."

Madeleine dismissed his apologetic tone with a tilt of her hand. "Don't worry about it. On the phone a couple of days ago, she was so distraught I couldn't make out which of the disappearances affected her most, the man or the money."

"I take it from what you say that he's vanished?" The disapproving inflection in his voice was back.

"Yep. Into thin air, but I'm sure with a little digging we can find him. Mum insists it's all a misunderstanding, but something tells me he's done it before. I'm using some of my contacts at work to see if I can find out anymore, because I don't think she's telling me everything."

"Something she said or just intuition?" He cut her some cheese and placed it on a plate in front of her.

"I'm not sure." She sipped some wine, pondering his question. "I keep thinking there's something she said previously that makes me think it's worse, but I can't remember what it was. I hate the feeling when you know the answer is staring you in the face and yet you just can't quite reach out and grab it."

He reached out and gently touched her brow, smoothing her hair away from her face. "Relax, chérie, don't frown. You'll recall it more clearly if you stop fighting with your mind, n'est-ce pas?" Madeleine resisted the temptation to turn her cheek towards his sensuous caress, to rekindle some of the warmth they'd shared that afternoon.

"Perhaps you're right. It's so frustrating." She saw a sparkle in his eye. "What did I say?"

"I do not understand. What do you mean?" He feigned innocence and concentrated on cutting a piece of cheese, but Madeleine knew she'd said something that amused him.

"You're laughing at me."

He smiled and sat back, stretching one arm out to touch the back of Madeleine's chair. He seemed so at ease, whilst the tension building inside her was palpable as memories of their kiss earlier this afternoon flooded her thoughts.

"No, I would never laugh at you, but the memory makes me smile." She watched as he swirled his wine. The red liquid coated the glass with each tip of his hand as he decided whether or not to tell her. He lifted the glass to his mouth and swallowed the last of its contents, drawing her attention to the tanned neck she'd placed her lips on just a few hours ago.

"Today, when I first saw you, you were kicking the car."

She groaned and hid her head in her hands in mortification.

"Don't be embarrassed." He touched her hand, pulling at her fingers to reveal her face. "It summed up the day I was having. I even thought about getting out and joining in."

Madeleine's head snapped up. "Seriously?"

"Bien sûr. When you mentioned your frustration a moment ago, it reminded me of this afternoon." He looked so sincere Madeleine was almost convinced he meant it.

"So what ruined your day?" She was keen to take the spotlight off her own embarrassing actions.

"Besides having to rescue une naïade?" A glint in his eye told her he was teasing her. "About fifty million gallons of water—you see, we have synergy running through our problems."

She gave him a questioning glance.

"A cargo ship sank last night. The crew was saved. Unfortunately for me the containers weren't. That's what the call was about this afternoon. When I left the office earlier, contingency plans were in place, but it seems there were still other issues to consider."

"Oh no, that's awful." She imagined the terror for those on board. "Do you know how it happened?"

He shrugged. "I'm not sure. I think the weather was bad and then something was not right with the ship, but now the problem is to minimise the disruption. Otherwise we have contracts that will be delayed."

"What was on the boat?"

"For us it was mainly chips for specialist industrial

computers, the type that can withstand high or low temperatures. The chips were to complete an order due to go to Australia. With luck, it will still leave the factory in time."

Seizing the opportunity to try and find out more about Jean-Luc, Madeleine quizzed him further, hoping she appeared interested and not interrogative.

"So what do you do? Logistics, supply chain, or are you made by your evil boss to test out the computers under extreme conditions?" She tried to interject a note of humour into her voice.

He smiled back wolfishly at her. "I am the evil boss." He leaned closer, waggling his eyebrows like a villain from a silent movie.

"Oh, sorry, I mean, I should have known." Her embarrassment, along with colour flooding her cheeks, returned yet again. So much for finding out more about him, Sherlock. She couldn't even follow the obvious clues like the expensive car and a chateau as his home. For crying out loud, he was going to think she was an idiot.

"Don't be. I'm very proud of how much my company has achieved." He reached out to tuck a stray strand of hair she'd dislodged behind her ear. "We're one of the top manufacturers in our field and still expanding despite the recession. In fact, the Australian deal is a new market for us, which is why I am so keen to complete the order on time, regardless of a little water, ma naïade." He held her hand, unconsciously tracing the palm lines with his fingers as if they were rivulets of water.

From the way he enthusiastically spoke about his business, Madeleine couldn't imagine anything would dare stand in his way as he described some of the intricacies of the machines they developed. She listened intently, hypnotised by his soft French accent and fascinated as she discovered more about the man who'd built a successful multinational company in less than ten years.

As the conversation moved back to more general topics, Madeleine yawned.

"Boring you, am I?" The amusement in his eyes belied his indignant tone.

She smiled, sheepishly attempting to hide a second yawn. "I think the last few days are starting to catch up with me." Madeleine rose. "Thank you again for rescuing me, and be sure to tell Danielle dinner was fantastic..." Her words drifted off as she glanced into Jean-Luc's eyes as he stood up to escort her to the door. The desire blazing from their dark depths was impossible to miss, and Madeleine's mouth went dry as the nervousness from the car earlier that day returned, her tiredness forgotten in an instant.

"Thank you for making my dinner much more enjoyable, than sitting here in silence by myself with only my computer for company." His French accent lingered around the word enjoyable and the room temperature jumped up a notch. Jean-Luc leaned forward, his face just inches from hers. "Bon nuit." Then he captured her lips in a soft kiss that caused an explosion of tingling sensations across them. Wow. Her last coherent thought was that her memory really hadn't done their previous embrace justice.

When he moved his hand up to hold the back of her head and deepen the kiss, Madeleine gave herself up to the wantonness that engulfed her as Jean-Luc pulled her body closer to his, leaving her in no doubt as to the depth of his arousal. "You taste so sweet, ma petite naïade," he sighed against her lips, before capturing them once more to explore their softness.

The rasp of his tongue as he plundered her mouth and the scent of his aftershave filled Madeleine's senses as the tide of desire that had smouldered all night rose up within her and she returned his kiss. She reached upwards, her fingers lightly gripping his arms, relishing the feeling of strength underneath his shirt sleeves.

As the embrace intensified, her hands carried on their exploration into his thick, silky hair. A soft moan escaped from her as she felt Jean-Luc caress her body, his thumb circling her taut, erect nipple. Easing her away from him a fraction, he continued to kiss his way down her neck to the hollow of her collar-bone, pulling her cardigan away from her shoulders to reveal more skin, taking his time to savour every inch he uncovered.

Encouraging him to replace his mouth where his hands had been moments before, Madeleine pulled his head down further, gasping when his lips found their target through the fabric of the borrowed dress. Heat shot to her core as Jean-Luc shifted their position to place a well-muscled thigh between her legs, and it was all Madeleine could do not to wrap her own leg around his to draw him in closer. The anticipation of what might come simmered inside her.

The hard edge of the table jarred into Madeleine's consciousness as she leaned back. Her eyes snapped open, swiftly bringing her back to reality, if only momentarily. Jean-Luc leisurely made his way back to her lips, before placing his hands on her behind to lift her up onto the table, stepping in to fill the gap between her thighs.

He smiled as he took in Madeleine's surprise at being manoeuvred, held her gaze for a second, and then lowered his head to continue his exploration. Once again Madeleine was lost in a sea of sensations. Her hands roamed freely across his back and downwards, pulling him closer, adjusting her thighs to accommodate his hips.

Jean-Luc responded with a muffled groan as he bit into her neck in playful response. His hands promised revenge as one touched her breast and the other pulled her tighter to the hard length of his erection, driving Madeleine insane for more. As her fingers reached for his belt, Jean-Luc held them away, regret in his eyes.

"We should stop." His husky voice barely registered through the haze of desire. "Go to bed, Madeleine. There's no bell to save you this time, and there is only so much I can stand. I promised you I'd behave myself tonight, but if we carry on like this, I might just break that promise."

CHAPTER 4

He never tired of the view from up here. The road twisted and turned as it rose into the hills, and then on this last corner it dropped steeply into the deep valley below, the wide river flowing steadily at its base. He could drive the route blindfolded he knew every curve so intimately, every gear change so precisely.

Days like this were rare, and Jean-Luc savoured each moment away from his hectic schedule. He loved to drive the powerful sports car. Taking risks, with fast cars at any rate, was something he'd stopped the moment Chantal became his responsibility. The Ferrari was an indulgence for the open road, when he needed an escape from the claustrophobic SUV and chauffeured company car.

He used the car's natural engine braking to manoeuvre it along the winding road. When he came to a straight section, he glanced across briefly at Madeleine, who was seated beside him. Wisps of hair teased out from underneath her hat as the wind whipped lightly across her face. With a faint smile on her lips, she looked happy and relaxed for the first time since they'd met yesterday afternoon.

A potentially awkward breakfast had been avoided this morning by the distraction of Danielle working in the kitchen. Instead it had been a friendly affair, and Madeleine had seemed genuinely pleased at his insistence of a day out exploring the local scenery. He smiled as he remembered her startled look when he pulled up outside the front door.

"I cannot show you the beautiful countryside wrapped up in the cocoon of a car I drove yesterday, can I?" He walked round to open the door. A sweet hibiscus scent floated up as she slid down into the low-slung seat, reminding him of the night before. Today was going to be a long day if he didn't rein in his thoughts.

"Sorry." She grinned impishly at him, and for a moment he struggled to remember what he'd said. "I just wasn't expecting something quite so... I don't know... Red."

"Red." He pretended to be confused by her answer, unable to resist teasing her as she squirmed prettily in the seat.

"Well, you know."

"No, chérie, I don't."

"It's just with the chateau looking so majestic and stories of Raphael and Danielle and a simple country upbringing, I wasn't expecting something quite so..."

"Red?" he supplied, mocking her.

Suddenly, she straightened up and turned to him, her green eyes filled with determination. She probably didn't mean it to, but it gave away another side to her character. This was the Madeleine who faced challenges head on, who resisted the urge to be intimidated by her surroundings, including him. He found it surprisingly endearing.

"Actually, I wanted to say flashy." Her cheeks took on a pink hue. "A discreet Mercedes or a Porsche, maybe, but I wasn't expecting a Ferrari."

"I'm sorry to disappoint you." He feigned hurt as he sat behind the wheel. "I must warn you, though, that I have a helicopter, too." And he gunned the car down the driveway, his mood lighter than it had been in a long while.

Madeleine brought him back to the present when she reached across and touched his arm to point out a buzzard gliding along beside them before swooping down into the gorge below. Her hand no longer remained there, but the heat from it left an imprint behind. Not for the first time in the last twelve hours, he wondered what would have happened last night if he hadn't promised her she would be safe with him.

It took all of his strength to resist her allure, and a long, cold shower before bed did nothing to drench the fire. But today—today was different. There were no promises, and he had no intention of making any. He'd never met someone who intrigued him so much, and he wasn't about to let the opportunity to learn more about Madeleine slip through his fingers.

At the bottom of the gorge, Jean-Luc drove the car through a medieval arch, pulling into a parking spot in the town square. It was already hot, and he worried about Madeleine's pale complexion as they wandered around the town's narrow streets, admiring the architecture and the stalls of a local market. When they made it back to where they started, he took her hand and led her to sit under the awning of a restaurant.

"So what happened to Raphael? You never said last night."

"Raph?" He twisted his mouth in a wry smile. Madeleine constantly turned the conversation away from herself. "Raphael went into the property market. Now he travels the world, pleasing himself. We meet when we can and talk about old times, but I think he prefers his playboy lifestyle to the one his parents would rather he keep. His antics are well known in the village. They think of him as..." Jean-Luc searched for the right word.

"Un chaud lapin?"

He burst out laughing. "Tiens. You have not forgotten the French you learnt at school."

She kept a straight face and raised her hands in an exaggerated Gallic shrug. "Well, not the important phrases."

"I'm quite intrigued to know how a phrase associated with the sexual prowess of our presidents came up in lessons."

"I used to live in France, well, for a summer, anyway. A friend of my mother's loaned her an apartment. I was four at the time, but a lot of the French I learnt stuck."

"You learnt chaud lapin when you were four?" The woman was incorrigible.

She leaned in closer to him, mouth tilted upward in a soft smile, her breath teasing the side of his neck. "No, that phrase came later."

The desire reflected in her eyes as he turned his head made Jean-Luc swallow hard before capturing her lips with his. Heat flooded through him as she matched his swift, insistent, and unrelenting assault on her mouth.

Their waitress flounced past a couple of times, and Jean-Luc swore. Yet again, he'd chosen the wrong place to start a seduction. Did he enjoy torturing himself, or was it part of a larger conspiracy against him?

"Time to make our choice before she starts slamming down the cutlery between us." The tilt of Madeleine's smile as she whispered against his lips made him itch to kiss her again, but reluctantly he drew back.

He couldn't remember the last time he'd enjoyed a leisurely lunch. Seated in the light shade, Madeleine told him a little about her life in London. Or at least a version of it. Like the sun glimmering through a crack in the awning, catching the glints of chestnut and bronze in her hair, it was only the highlights.

Not that he was in a position to criticise. After Maman's death, he learnt it was safer to say nothing, give no details away, no matter how innocent. The papers soon got bored and moved on to their next victim. It was the actions of so-called friends that cut deeper.

"What about you? Have you always been destined to be an electronics magnate?" Predictably, she turned the focus back to him.

"I was lucky. At university, I was interested in computers and industry, and I saw an opportunity to combine the two and carve out a niche. It was a very small operation at first, but as our reputation grew, it developed into something even I didn't envisage."

"Do you still enjoy it as much as when you first started?"

"Yes. More so now because I get to do things the way I want them done, not dictated to by banks or investors like I was in the beginning."

"Master of your own destiny." She smiled and gave him a wink, tipping her head to study him some more. "I think it suits you."

"It's the only way to get want you want." Playing up to the moment, he leaned in to steal a quick kiss from her lips.

"On y va. Let's go." He stood in one fluid movement, tossed some notes down onto the table, and took her hand to help her up. "You haven't seen the most fascinating part of this town."

As they went further underground, Madeleine shivered. The dark, damp cold was a stark contrast to the sweltering heat at the restaurant. Jean-Luc drew her closer to him. An electric charge flowed from the point where his hand touched her elbow, his strong fingers curving round her forearm.

She stumbled on the uneven path as it wove its way through the maze of underground caves filled with stalactites and stalagmites.

"Careful, the ground is slippery." He steadied her, his hold on her tightening.

She listened to him as he translated the tour guide's speech, understanding enough French to realise Jean-Luc embellished the stories with tales of ghosts and superstitions. He whispered huskily to her in the dark, his voice vibrating against the back of her ear, causing her nipples to tighten and her stomach to do somersaults in response.

Enchanted by the magic of the place and hypnotised by the sound of his deep, seductive tone, Madeleine let herself be swept along by Jean-Luc's stories and gave up trying to fathom if there was any basis of truth in them.

"You see the red stain in the stone there, where the two rocks meet?"

Madeleine strained to see in the dim light.

"It's said two lovers fought here. She cracked her head on the stone, and distraught at his mistake he drowned himself in the deep pool that the ripples flow into over there."

"You don't think it might just be iron washed down from up above?" She glanced up at him, but the expression in his face didn't match the humour in hers.

Even in the darkness she could see the haunted look in his eyes. He shook his head and pursed his lips. "No, it was an all-consuming passion destroying everything in its path."

"And what do you know of dark desires?"

"Perhaps more than you realise, ma naïade." He tilted his head down towards hers and kissed her slowly, lingering, deepening the kiss when the rest of the tour moved on to the next cave. When his shoulders relaxed under her fingertips, she realised he'd taken a solace from her lips she didn't even know she'd offered. Her resolve not to get involved wavered with every hour spent in Jean-Luc's company.

She placed a hand on his cheek and drew away, searching in his eyes for an explanation, but he blinked and the sardonic, sexy glint she was used to seeing returned, sending a thrill down her spine. She sighed inwardly. It was foolish to resist him when her body had already made up its mind.

By the time they arrived for dinner at a restaurant on the drive home, Madeleine conceded defeat against the charms of the beautiful French countryside, the sunshine, and the Frenchman himself.

She sipped her wine and glanced at the bottle before looking out over the terrace. A Bergerac, how fitting. She'd hardly thought of her mother and her machinations all day, but it still irked her. How the hell did several hundred thousand euros disappear into thin air?

Her neck muscles tightened, along with her nerves, and

stress started to seep into her bones. She took another sip of wine, determined not to waste another moment on her mother.

From their high vantage point, Madeleine could see for miles. Content to continue his earlier role as tour guide, she listened attentively, mesmerised by Jean-Luc's accent and the timbre of his voice. She was so wrapped up in hearing about his love for the region and its history, enjoying the way his expressive hands added depth to his words, she didn't even notice their meal.

By the time he'd finished telling her about the area, the vista had faded into the dusk. Beyond the soft lights of the terrace, darkness surrounded them, creating a magical air to the evening. A warm breeze tickled the back of her neck, bringing with it the scent of rosemary and lavender.

Jean-Luc reached out and took her hand, twining their fingers together. He rubbed his thumb over her forefinger before releasing it and reaching for his glass. "So have you ever lived anywhere else in Europe?"

"I spent a summer in Italy one year. That was Frederico."

"Frederico?" Jean-Luc almost choked on his wine.

"Hmmm?" She frowned at his perplexed expression, before the realisation of his confusion dawned on her. "Oh, sorry, I remember most of my life by my mother's romances."

"There were that many?" He sounded slightly more relaxed.

"A few. In my mind Frederico was the worst. Mostly I didn't get to see them, only the countries they lived in. My mother only introduced me with feigned forgetfulness when she'd had enough and didn't want to be the one who broke it off."

"What was wrong with Frederico?"

"Ahh, it didn't go quite the way my mother planned. Rather than being put off by an unwanted daughter, he chased me, too." Jean-Luc's face took on a thunderous frown. She reached out a hand to reassure him. "I was nearly nineteen at the time. My mother hadn't realised how much I grown up that last year at boarding school."

"Really?" His incredulous tone made it clear he still wasn't impressed with her mother's choice of friends.

At his almost imperceptible nod encouraging her to continue, she took a deep breath to calm her rising temper at remembering the situation.

"We had quite a show down. I told her I'd had enough of impossible situations and I would no longer do her dirty work for her every time she wanted to break up a relationship. She had to do it herself, and if she couldn't, then she and Frederico deserved each other."

His eyebrows shot up at the forcefulness of Madeleine's response. "What happened?"

"I booked a flight back to the UK. By the time I left, Frederico had also packed his bags, and Mum was planning her next adventure. I told myself from this moment on my mother was on her own." Madeleine took a sip of wine and grimaced. "Inevitably it wasn't the case."

"Hence you are here in France."

"France, yes, and several other places in between. After Frederico she started coming up with elaborate excuses as to why she needed me to come and visit her."

"Perhaps she and Chantal should get together. They both sound like the perfect manipulators of family emotions."

Madeleine raised her lips in half a smile at his joke and shook her head.

"I don't think that would be such a good idea. Who knows what might happen? Left to her own devices, my mother is bad enough. Once, under the pretext of her passport being destroyed, she made me rush out to Greece with a photocopy of the original and her birth certificate."

"You couldn't courier them?"

"How would you feel if, on top of all the upheaval, my identity was stolen, too?" Madeleine mimicked her mother. "To give her some credit, when I arrived the passport had genuinely been destroyed, but of course there was the inevitable boyfriend to dispatch, too."

"I'm sure I could match your tales with some of the ways Chantal manages to run rings round me. She's currently in Paris. As normal she's overspent her allowance doing some retail therapy, I think you call it, in a fit of pique over an argument with a friend."

"Boyfriend?"

"No. I thank the stars that where men are concerned, she's totally immune."

"Wise girl. But at least she has youth as an excuse. My mother's supposed to be setting me an example, not the other way round. The worst time was somewhere deep in South America."

A sly grin came over Jean-Luc's face. "Manu National Park?"

"Yes, how did you guess?"

Jean-Luc shrugged.

"Anyway, long story short, we got on the plane by the skin of our teeth with nothing but the clothes we wore and our passports. I used all the cash we had to bribe our way out. Twenty minutes into the flight, my mother turned on the charm and persuaded someone to buy us drinks."

Jean-Luc was trying to be polite and appear consoling at her obvious annoyance, but he could barely smother his laughter.

"You may laugh, but now that I think about it, he turned out to be failed romance number seven after Mum contacted him again in London, ostensibly to repay the money he'd so generously lent."

Unable to help himself any longer, Jean-Luc's face broke into a grin. "But it's priceless. You are managing to make Chantal seem like an angel by comparison." He held his hand against her cheek, and the laughter died on his lips. His eyes turned serious, holding her gaze as her breath caught in her throat. "I'm glad you still rescue her." The softly spoken words caused a shiver to float up Madeleine's spine.

His hand was warm as it took hers and turned it over, bringing her palm to his lips for a slow kiss. A flame deep within Madeleine rose up and refused to be dampened down. Her annoyance with her mother forgotten, she lost herself to Jean-Luc's seductive touch as the sweet scent of twilight closed in and engulfed them.

THE CLOCK ON THE DASHBOARD SHOWED TWO MINUTES TO midnight as they pulled into the courtyard. The moment the car stopped, the door to the chateau flew open, and Danielle ran down the steps. Her face etched with worry, she launched into an emotional tirade, too fast for Madeleine to understand.

The tension in Jean-Luc was palpable as he stepped out of the car. The relaxed, elegant Frenchman was gone. In his place stood a cold, hard stranger, his jaw tight, fists clenched as he listened to Danielle before questioning her in clipped tones. His ruthless manner would have most people cowering, but the housekeeper didn't even flinch.

Instead, she begged imploringly at Jean-Luc. "Elle a besoin de toi."

She needs you, Madeleine translated. Who needed him and why at this hour?

He sighed. "Bien."

The unease between the two lessened a little as the housekeeper released her grip on Jean-Luc's forearm, but ratcheted up inside Madeleine as she took a step closer.

He turned at her movement.

"I'm sorry." His autocratic air denied the apology. "Something has come up. I need to go back out. I'll see you tomorrow at breakfast."

Madeleine watched as he got back in the car and sped up the driveway, his red tail lights disappearing into the warm, dark night.

So much for romance. The least he could have done was look a bit more disappointed at the abrupt end to their day. Instead, she'd swear he'd forgotten all about her the instant Danielle had opened the front door.

She blew out an exasperated breath and followed the housekeeper back into the chateau.

Even the splendour of her room didn't ease her irritation as she flung herself across the bed and reached for her mobile. At least now that the weather had improved, the signal had returned.

She glanced at the screen. Three messages. The first was her mother. Great, as if the evening couldn't get any better. Perhaps she'd save listening to it until tomorrow. She skipped to the next one and was cheered to hear Kathy's voice wondering how France compared to the Caribbean.

Knowing she would still be at the office, Madeleine texted her back: *No contest. Weather unpredictable and so are the men. Will call soon x.*

The third message from Jeff in the fraud department at work was more cryptic.

"Hi Maddie. I did a bit of digging on Charles Fairfax Jackson. His name flagged up with a bank in Australia. It seems as if they've been looking for him for some time in connection with a possible fraud. I've sent you an email with the details. If your mum wants her money back, then I suggest you move fast. There are plenty of other people queueing up in front of her."

After reading Jeff's email, Madeleine couldn't shake the same feeling she'd had last night. Charles Jackson had first appeared on the scene several months ago when he'd moved into her mother's apartment. Having seen it all before, she wasn't concerned. Her mother was always careful to make sure that no one else had access to her money, or so Madeleine had thought.

Pushing herself off the bed, she headed for the shower. Perhaps she'd remember what it was that nagged at the back of her mind after a good night's rest.

Her phone beeped as she climbed into bed with Kathy's response: *The best ones never are.*

She was as big a push over for romance as my mother. Rearranging the covers, she punched her pillow as one enigmatic, impossibly handsome Frenchman strayed into her thoughts before turning off the light.

Irritation still lingered at his abrupt departure, but the curiosity as to what the mysterious urgency was all about was stronger. Once again she was forced to realise she knew nothing about the man. She'd have asked Danielle, but there was no point, because she was too loyal to Jean-Luc. The answer would have been as noncommittal as every other conversation she'd tried to have with her.

What was it that made him change the subject rapidly every time he talked about his mother? Last time he'd distracted her with just a kiss. Giving into temptation was one thing, particularly when the packaging was so irresistible, but she knew where she wasn't welcome. Tomorrow she'd find a hotel until her car was fixed.

Madeleine counted possible excuses for his sudden departure instead of sheep. Her last coherent thought as she drifted off to sleep was that he probably had a deranged wife locked away in one of the turrets.

CHAPTER 5

The alleyway split in two. Should she turn left or right? Behind her loomed a danger she couldn't quite distinguish, but her sanity depended on her escaping its capture. She stopped running for a moment and became aware of screaming. Who was screaming? Her? No, this was outside the dream.

She sat bolt upright in bed. The terrified screams of a woman assaulted her ears and sent a chill down her spine. The sound was definitely coming from within the chateau.

Madeleine leapt out of bed and sped across the room. She opened the door and caught a glimpse of Danielle entering a room further down the hallway. The screams continued, punctuated by brief moments of eerie quietness as presumably whoever it was filled their lungs with oxygen ready for the next ear-piercing noise.

The only other people in the chateau were herself and Jean-Luc, so who on earth was wailing like a murder had been committed? With only the dim light from the lamps on the stairway for guidance, she forced herself to take a step into the darkened corridor.

Her heart thumped in her throat. If this was a horror movie, she'd be shouting at the TV for the heroine not to follow the screams.

Jean-Luc appeared at the top of the stairs. Madeleine gasped and jumped at his sudden appearance. He still wore the same clothes from earlier. Taking long strides down the hallway, he barely paused when he saw her.

"Go back to bed, Madeleine. There's nothing you can do."

The command was curt and dismissive. She opened her mouth to ask who it was, but the tiredness in his face swayed her into giving a small nod of acceptance. He didn't stop to see what she did, but hurried along the hallway and went through the same doorway Danielle had entered moments ago.

She stood in the corridor, her heart still beating rapidly. Jean-Luc's voice filtered through the closed door. As he spoke in low, soothing tones, the terrifying echoes that haunted the stone walls of the chateau subsided. Madeleine breathed a sigh of relief and turned to creep back to her room.

Not bothering to turn on the light, she crossed the room and stepped out onto the balcony. The night was lit by a blaze of stars streaking across the sky, and a glow on the horizon announced the moon's impending arrival. She leaned on the railing. The sound of the crickets and frogs singing in the grass below was almost deafening, but after the screams the monotonous melody was tranquil and comforting.

What had she got herself into? Tonight proved she knew

little more after spending the day with Jean-Luc than she had the night before. Aside from the fact that the more she kissed him, the more she wanted him, which rankled. Torrid affairs were her mother's domain.

Which was how she'd gotten into this mess.

Five days ago when her mother had called, Madeleine had pictured her at the other end of the line, her petite figure, face beautifully made up, blond hair swept up in a chignon, and her heart had gone out to her. Despite their tempestuous relationship over the years, hearing her mother cry down the phone roused her protective instincts. Without a second thought she agreed to come out to France.

Until she'd finished the call and realised yet again she'd been manipulated into doing exactly what her mother wanted and had cancelled her Caribbean trip. She could have kicked herself. Still could, for that matter.

And here she was. Ironically, as lost and unsure as to what to do next as she had been when Jean-Luc had found her on the road.

JEAN-LUC RAISED A HAND TO MADELEINE'S DOOR AND PAUSED. He owed her an explanation, but a wave of helplessness hit him in the gut, choking him as he thought of Chantal now asleep across the hallway. Moving his hand away from the door, he ran it through his hair and sighed. He needed to get a grip on his emotions.

It ate away at him that no matter how much he protected Chantal from the real world, there was nothing he could do to defend her from her dreams. That she never remembered them was a small mercy.

Jean-Luc took a deep breath and exhaled slowly. One day

she would find peace with her demons, and they could both move on with their lives.

He knocked softly and pushed open the door. A warm breeze brushed past him, drawing his gaze to the balcony.

Jean-Luc's pulse picked up at the sight of Madeleine bathed in moonlight. She'd twisted round at the sound of the door opening. The action outlined the tip of her breast and shapely behind to perfection through the translucent fabric of her camisole and shorts.

He hadn't noticed what she was wearing earlier. He'd been too concerned over Chantal's screams. Now he let his gaze roam over Madeleine, careful to take in every detail. She looked as graceful as a ballerina and as desirable as a siren. A craving coursed through his blood. He wanted her more than he had anyone in a long time, maybe ever, and his fingers tingled with the need to reach out and touch her.

Then he noted the wariness in her face and groaned inwardly. How did he explain without creating an atmosphere of sorrow and pity that he just wanted to escape for a few hours?

He tempered down his lust-filled thoughts and strove to speak in an even tone. "I'm sorry. It was my sister. She has these dreams..." he offered by way of explanation, knowing it was no explanation at all.

"Is she okay?" Jean-Luc couldn't see Madeleine's eyes, but he heard the concern in her voice. He rarely discussed Chantal, and he sure as hell wasn't going to now. Not with Madeleine wearing next to nothing and his blood about to boil over from the heat he sensed they would generate together.

"She is sleeping. Danielle will stay with her for the rest of the night in case they return."

Madeleine turned back to stare out into the night, and Jean-Luc stepped into the room, closing the door behind him. As his eyes adjusted to the darkness, he saw Madeleine was watching wispy clouds float across the sky, backlit by the silver light of the moon.

This room, like his, overlooked the valley beyond the chateau grounds. The river wound its way through the hillside, and on nights like this he thought it was one of the most beautiful vistas in the world. But tonight, with Madeleine in the foreground, that view was immeasurably improved.

He walked over to join her on the balcony. "You couldn't sleep?" The warm scent of the night merged with Madeleine's own sweet fragrance, and Jean-Luc breathed it in, filling his senses. Arousal rushed back with a vengeance.

"No. Strange, isn't it?" She tilted her head and gave him a mocking look, dousing his ardour and reminding him how he'd nearly had a heart attack this evening when she'd mentioned Frederico. For one moment he'd thought Madeleine was discussing past lovers when he was doing his best to seduce her. She held him continually off balance, and the sadistic side of him enjoyed it.

"What kept you awake?" Despite trying to temper down his lustful feelings, his voice was hoarse.

She regarded at him as if he was mad. Perhaps he was. This was starting to feel like insanity.

"It's not often a girl breaks down, gets rescued by a handsome stranger who takes her back to an imposing chateau where someone screams the place down in the middle of the night."

"So you think I'm handsome?" He took a step closer, willing his body to behave.

"I'm telling you I was too terrified to sleep, and all you take from the conversation is that I think you're hot?" A look of incredulity flitted across her face and she tried to move backwards, but he reached out and took her hand. Despite the warm evening, her skin was cool.

"But you are not terrified now, are you?" His voice sounded strained even to him, and unable to stop himself, Jean-Luc touched her neck with his other hand. "I can see from this erratic pulse here that it is not the sounds of the night that scare you, but I think you are still afraid of something. Your emotions or me?"

Madeleine lowered her head. Maybe he wasn't the only one who felt the madness. Gently he placed a hand on her cheek and raised her head. Green eyes, darkened with passion, stared back at him. "So, which is it?"

"Both." She sighed, leaning into his hand.

"Don't think, chérie, just feel." He pressed his lips to hers, coaxing her to respond. When her hands tugged on his shirt, pulling him closer, he deepened the kiss and lost himself to the pleasures of exploring the sweetness of her mouth.

Heat and passion took over his senses. The slow kisses of earlier in the day were nothing more than appetisers compared to this. He wanted to consume all of her. To be buried deep within her and release the sexual tension building between them. More than anything, he wanted to forget about the responsibilities of life and enjoy the moment with her.

He moved his mouth to nibble her neck and followed it to the fine outline of her collarbone. Tasting, kissing, and nipping, he gloried in Madeleine's reactions—sometimes a sigh, sometimes a gasp. The sensation of her nipples through the silky material of her nightwear as they hardened beneath his roaming hands sent his blood rushing south.

Sliding down the straps of her top, he took first one breast and then the other into his mouth, feasting on the soft flesh, teasing their pink tips. Madeleine's hands twisting in his hair to draw him closer drove him to new heights. If he wasn't careful, he'd be taking her right here on the balcony. He couldn't remember the last time someone made him want to give in to the loss of control.

He needed to slow himself down. Easing back a little, he blew a gentle breath across Madeleine's sensitive skin.

"So how long has your sister had nightmares?" Her voice cut through the haze of arousal like a bucket of cold water.

Mon Dieu, was she trying to kill him? Here he was, his erection painfully hard against her soft belly, her delightful body reacting to every touch of his hands, and she asked questions.

He took a deep breath and tried to refocus.

"Ever since my mother died." He straightened up and took her earlobe between his teeth, using his tongue to persuade her how it could perform on other areas of her body.

"Do you know what she dreams about?"

He continued down her neck in a bid to distract her from more probing questions, but her hands had paused in their own quest to undo his shirt and he knew Madeleine was waiting for his answer.

"Oui."

Jean-Luc pulled her close so she could feel the strength of his arousal. Her hips arched forward in response, and the movement bought a low groan from his lips. How did she manage to keep her head clear enough to ask questions when she had him tied up in knots? He wanted to drive her as wild as she made him, but he sensed Madeleine had still not finished what she wanted to say and he gently pulled back to give her a moment.

"You're not exactly full on with the answers, are you?" The huskiness of her voice gave away how much desire was affecting her. It was a small comfort, but he'd take it.

"I'm dealing with questions of my own, like what it would be like to kiss you here." He knelt to kiss her inner thigh slowly and deliberately, the softness of her skin against his stubble sending him into sensory overload. "Or how you'll react when I kiss you here?" His lips trailed further up her leg. "Or whether you'll make that sexy little sigh when my tongue touches you here."

He heard her gasp as his tongue rasped against the silky fabric at the juncture where her thighs met, and he smiled to himself, pleased that finally he had silenced the questions.

"Does she have them often?"

Merde. Jean-Luc stopped his exploration and gazed into her eyes, seeing a desire that matched his own.

"Do you really want to talk about my sister now?" He couldn't keep the derisive tone out of his voice, but when her whispered *no* reached his ears as she drew his head back, it was all the encouragement he needed to move aside the silk of her shorts with his tongue. She was so wet and hot it drove him crazy.

The sweet taste of her filled his senses as he licked and stroked her. He slid the satin material down her legs. The trembling of her thighs beneath his fingers made him tighten his grip. The sight of his tanned hands on her pale flesh excited him, pulling him to a deeper pleasure than he could ever remember experiencing. Free of her shorts, he moved her legs further apart and continued to feast his eyes and mouth on her unhindered. His tongue swirled around the swollen nub of her clitoris, sucking and nipping until she begged him for release.

He clasped the cheeks of her bottom with his hands and held her close as she bucked against him, her fingers digging into his shoulders as she climaxed. Her stifled cry shattering the silence. The depth of emotion she evoked in him with her ability to relinquish control so deeply tied a knot in his gut.

He pushed aside the unfamiliar reaction to continue his sensual assault on her body, deftly removing her top to expose her breasts fully to his touch. Jean-Luc adored the way Madeleine responded to him, inflaming his own desire further. When he could take no more, he swept her up and took her back into the room, placing her gently on the bed. He stood back for a moment and removed the rest of his clothing, admiring her naked form in the moonlight.

"Ma petite naïade, you entice me beyond what a normal man can stand."

Green eyes, heavy with desire, gazed back at him, and a slow smile crossed her lips.

"Ah, but you can see me any night of the week, and I'll even let you watch me bathe."

She rose onto her knees and reached for him. As her hand closed around his cock, Jean-Luc's breath caught in his throat, and he struggled to maintain control.

"Madeleine, you have to stop. I can't take anymore." He barely recognised his own voice.

"Then why wait?"

He didn't need any more encouragement. Snatching a condom from his trousers, Jean-Luc had it on and Madeleine underneath him in seconds. He caught her lips in a soft kiss as he entered her slowly, delighting in the warmth that wrapped around him as he pushed deep into her.

EVERY SENSORY NERVE WITHIN MADELEINE WAS ON HIGH ALERT, competing eagerly for Jean-Luc's sexual attention. Arms stretched out, their hands and lips entwined, her body became feverish as anticipation grew, arching of its own volition to meet his lips as they left a blazing trail across her skin.

The tickling of his chest hair as it brushed across her sensitive breasts was electrifying. She placed her mouth on his nipple, rolling her tongue around it, savouring the salty flavour. When she grazed the tight bud with her teeth, she was rewarded with a not-so-gentle bite to her neck that jolted her right to the core, making her cry out.

"Witch." Jean-Luc's deep voice sent reverberations of desire down her spine as he whispered in her ear. When he kissed the spot where his teeth had been, a deep sensation pooled low down within her, making her writhe with delight.

"What happened to the sprite?" Her hands swept over Jean-Luc's glistening skin as she continued to caress his chest, shoulders, and arms. Her lips and fingertips craved to trace the contours of his strong muscles beneath them.

"I made a mistake. You have so bewitched me that la naïade is too innocent." Black eyes bored into hers. The desire in them made Madeleine hold her breath in anticipation as Jean-Luc bent his head and took her lips in a searing kiss that drove her wild.

Firm hands pulled her legs around his waist, raising her

hips higher and allowing him to penetrate deeper. Madeleine revelled in the hardness that filled her, the pressure of his body as his thrusts splintered her into a million pieces. She relished the sensation as her inner muscles pulsated around him and he climaxed with a hoarse explosion of incomprehensible French.

Slowly, the silence returned. She could no longer hear her blood rushing through her body or feel her heartbeat pulsating in her neck. She opened her eyes and peered into Jean-Luc's inscrutable face. Was the unbridled passion she'd seen earlier just a figment of her imagination?

He kissed her anxieties away with a slow exploration of her face before rolling to his side and pulling her close, surrounding her body in the protective embrace of his arms.

Soothed by the sound of the crickets and the warm breeze floating over her skin, her eyes closed. As she drifted off to sleep, Madeleine realised that once again Jean-Luc had distracted her rather than answer her questions.

CHAPTER 6

Madeleine followed the sound of conversation to the kitchen. She recognised Jean-Luc's deep timbre, but not the lighter feminine voice intertwined with it. By the tone and the few words she could make out, it sounded like a well-run argument between guardian and ward, not brother and sister.

She pushed the door ajar. A slim figure with cropped blond hair and wearing a pink cotton cardigan sat with her back to Madeleine. Next to her, at the head of the table, was Jean-Luc, surrounded by a tablet, paperwork, and a cup of coffee. He stood and took a step towards Madeleine, blocking her entrance into the kitchen.

A jolt of apprehension struck her at his intense gaze, followed by a rush of excitement as he took a step forward, forcing her back into the hallway. The firm surface of the wall against her back halted her movement. She breathed in deeply, the scent of his sandalwood aftershave intoxicated her senses. Her heart rate spiked and arousal flooded through her as he placed his hands on either side of her and leaned in, trapping her beneath him.

The niggling doubt that perhaps he regretted last night was banished when his lips met hers. The soft pressure on her mouth as he coaxed her to open up to him sent her heartbeat spiralling out of control. Her hands longed to reacquaint themselves with his torso, but his own arms trapped them. Tasting him without touching his body was tantamount to torture.

A loud cough from the kitchen drew them apart.

"I'm sorry. I don't seem to be able to control myself around you." His mouth tilted into half a smile and he didn't look sorry at all as he released Madeleine from the delicious imprisonment of his hard body. "Come, I'll introduce you to Chantal. She's being her normal bratty self this morning." His voice grew louder on the latter half of the sentence.

"I can understand English, you know."

Madeleine smiled at the snarky reply from the other side of the door.

Chantal turned around as they entered the kitchen. She was every bit as exquisite as the rooms she decorated. Whereas Jean-Luc was dark from his eyes to his moods, Chantal was much fairer. Her blond hair cut in a pixie style only emphasised her delicate features, though the perfectly applied makeup didn't quite hide the shadows underneath her eyes.

"Chantal, Madeleine—Madeleine, my wayward sister Chantal," Jean-Luc offered by way of introduction.

Chantal put down her croissant and took Madeleine's hand. "Enchantée. Take no notice of my brother. He's just mad because I've had a good time in Paris, while he spends his days with his head stuck in a computer. Sometimes literally." She smiled at her own joke, but her hazel eyes remained sombre.

Madeleine glanced at Jean-Luc. His toast and coffee forgotten, he was totally absorbed in whatever he was reading on the tablet in front of him. He looked up and caught her staring. The heat in his eyes from a moment ago had gone, replaced by a calm, controlled facade. Presumably for his sister's benefit. She only hoped hers matched it.

As she turned her focus back to Chantal, Madeleine would swear she saw him wink at her, before his gaze went back to the computer screen, but his face gave nothing away.

"Sit down and help yourself to breakfast." Chantal waved a hand at the array of patisseries in front of her and the cafetière beside it. "Jean-Luc mentioned your car broke down?"

"Yes. I'm hoping when they call later it's something that can be fixed quickly, so I can stop intruding on your hospitality." She reached out and took a croissant and spoonful of jam, imagining the inches being added to her waistline just by inhaling the warm buttery smell. How Chantal stayed slim with a breakfast like this every morning was beyond her.

"Pas de problème, don't worry about it. It's so nice to have another female around here for companionship. Jean-Luc is so wrapped up in his work that I never get a chance to enjoy myself."

"Says the girl who has just come back from Paris." At his sardonic reply, Madeleine glanced over, but he didn't raise his head from the screen.

"Well, that's why I went. It's so boring here."

"You will be pleased to know then that I need to go into

the office today," he said, finally looking up. "So you can take charge of Madeleine and entertain her."

"No, there's no need," said Madeleine. Spending the day with Jean-Luc was one thing, but being entertained like she was an invited guest made her uncomfortable. "I'm sure I can find plenty to occupy myself here."

"Quoi!" shrieked Chantal. "Don't be ridiculous. Besides, there's a brocante I need to go to and we can take a wander through the market afterwards. I'll need some money."

Madeleine felt as if she was witnessing a mini-whirlwind as she tried to keep up with Chantal's train of thought. Still facing Madeleine, Chantal continued to rattle off a list of places they should visit, whilst her hand was outstretched behind her, aimed towards her brother. Chantal ignored his pointed expression as he pulled out a bundle of notes from his wallet and counted them off.

Perhaps he hadn't exaggerated when he said Chantal knew how to get around him, but she really couldn't let him pay.

"No, I insist. It's my treat. I need to pay my own way, and you've already done enough in rescuing me and letting me stay here."

Jean-Luc regarded her with amusement. "You may be able to pay your way, but believe me, you won't be able to afford Chantal." He stood and slipped his tablet into a brief-case beside him and took Madeleine's hand as if was the most natural thing in the world. "Chantal, when you've finished dragging Madeleine through the shops, drop her off at the office."

He dropped a kiss on the top of Chantal's head and pulled Madeleine through a door at the other end of the kitchen and out into a square stone courtyard.

"I'm sorry to leave you like this, but it's unavoidable." He halted their progress along the covered walkway and dragged her hand up to his chest, pulling her close. "Don't look so dazed, chérie. I promise I won't abandon you like your mother. It's only for a few hours."

Madeleine laughed at his teasing and pulled her hand back. "It's not that. It's just this chateau is like a rabbit warren, and the moment I think I've seen it all another section appears. Where does the door over there lead to?" She pointed across the courtyard to an oak door that stood to one side of what appeared to be an old stable block.

"It's my mother's studio. It's not been used since she died." His tone turned sombre and Madeleine regretted asking, but if he chose not to tell her what the big secret was, then he could hardly be mad at her for asking the wrong questions.

A wry smile crossed his lips as if he'd guessed her thoughts, but he only shrugged in response and continued on to the garage.

Damn the man. One minute she was going up in flames, the next she was left out in the cold.

He paused as he opened the door to the SUV and gave a resigned sigh. "Take care of Chantal."

Her annoyance with him melted when she saw a little of his impassive facade crack.

"She's all bravado, but after nights like the last one, she needs a little..."

"TLC?"

"Oui. TLC." He reached out and placed a warm hand on her cheek. The gesture was simple, but Madeleine felt some-thing inexplicable pass between them.

"I'll explain when we have more time, I promise. Until I

do, it's probably best you steer clear of talking about my mother." With that intriguing comment, he got in the car and drove off.

CHANTAL DROPPED MADELEINE OFF AT THE FACTORY LATER that afternoon. Jean-Luc's PA greeted her and explained he would arrive in a few minutes, leaving her to wait in his office.

Declining the offer of coffee, Madeleine sat down in one of the leather chairs in the corner and picked up an electronics magazine from the coffee table. As she flicked through to the contents, she spied a feature on Jean-Luc.

Madeleine opened the magazine at the corresponding page to find Jean-Luc's enigmatic face staring back at her, the factory floor a blur in the background. Tracing her fingers over his features, Madeleine wondered when it was that her feelings had changed from attraction to something deeper. She was interested in everything he did and wished her French was slightly better to be able to understand the article.

Careful, next thing she knew she'd be dropping everything just to be at his side. Disgusted with herself for being as pathetic as her mother, she threw the magazine back down on the table.

"Bad review?" Startled by Jean-Luc's voice, Madeleine turned around and saw the humour in his eyes.

"Just a typical article about some businessman who mistakes luck for his entrepreneurial skill." She deliberately faked a haughty air.

"You doubt my abilities?" Jean-Luc pulled an affronted

face, but Madeleine knew he had too much confidence in himself to take her seriously.

"I'll let you know."

"In that case, I demand a chance to exonerate myself. Before we leave, I'll give you the tour. On y va." He held the door open for her to pass, the consummate businessman in front of his PA, until she passed him and he whispered. "You'll pay for that comment later." She hoped so.

Madeleine knew the tour was a delaying tactic, but she was prepared to wait. Whatever Jean-Luc had to tell her obviously weighed heavily on his mind.

He led her down to the ground floor. A maze of steel rollers conveying large plastic trays weaved their way across the different sections. A small gang of workers continually added computer parts into the containers.

"Each tub will contain every component needed to complete the hardware element for the computer before being passed to the assembly engineers," he explained.

As they walked through, most people took no notice of him. Jean-Luc was clearly a regular on the assembly floor and not just a nameplate on an office door. He stopped and drew someone aside to speak privately with them. As he walked away, Jean-Luc gave the worker's shoulder a sympathetic squeeze.

"Not working hard enough?"

"I was asking him how his mother was. His father died last month after a long illness." Jean-Luc didn't expand further, but in that instant Madeleine realised Jean-Luc didn't only take care of Chantal. His protective instincts took in everyone who relied on him. Including her.

After they finished the tour, Jean-Luc took her back up to his office. The factory itself was a low industrial building, with the assembly floor on the ground level and the offices above. Unlike the chateau, it was an ultra modern, functional, steel and glass affair. Jean-Luc's office in the corner was closed off from the rest of the building, but had far-reaching views across the outskirts of the town.

"I need to collect a couple of things, and then we can leave." Jean-Luc held the door open for Madeleine to pass through before closing it again.

"Take a seat. I won't be a minute." He gestured back to the couch where she'd been sitting earlier and went round to the other side of his desk and clicked a button on the computer. The magazine was still on the coffee table where she'd left it.

"So are you often the centrefold for business magazines?"

He glanced up from the screen, amusement in his eyes. "I'm frequently in the business pages, if that's what you mean. I'm not sure about the centrefold remark. Isn't that considered sexist?"

"Relax, it was meant to be. I wanted to see what you said."

"And?"

Madeleine pretended to study the picture some more, holding it out at arm's length, turning it to different angles.

"I don't think the picture is sexy at all." She was sure her nose grew at the blatant lie. "Not with that tie."

"I said sexist." He smiled, and his eyes took on a dangerous glint. "What's wrong with the tie?"

"It's boring, blue, and narrow. Hardly says bold risk taker or dynamic entrepreneur."

"It reflects the man that's wearing it. I'm neither of those. I like to think the company's success speaks for my character, not my clothes."

"Ahh, but clothes maketh the man."

"I don't think that's what Shakespeare meant, but from now on I'll always consult you on my choice of ties." He turned his attention back to the computer.

Madeleine sat patiently while Jean-Luc tapped on the keyboard, the silence stretching out as the awareness between them grew.

"So do you often pose for pictures like this?" She tried to portray an innocent expression on her face, knowing he would look up the moment the words left her lips.

"Why do I feel, chérie, like we're having some kind of double entendre conversation that seems to be reversed?"

Madeleine grinned at him. "I was trying to work out how to ask what you thought about sex in the office."

Without breaking their gaze, Jean-Luc was up and standing in front of her almost immediately.

"Well, if you want to find out what I think about sex in the office, you only needed to ask."

A thrill of desire flowed through her as he dropped to his knees, his hands already sliding up her skirt.

"Okay. Have you ever had sex in this office?"

"No." He lent forward to place a kiss on her inner thigh. His hands reached behind her to slide her forward in the chair and closer to him.

"Have you ever had sex in an office?"

He lifted his head and raised an eyebrow. "I'm not going to answer that one." He continued his path up the inside of her leg, his tongue making swirling patterns on her soft skin.

"I'll take it as a yes, then."

His hands reached up to quickly divest her of her underwear.

"Madeleine." His lack of patience was evident in his tone. "Has anyone ever told you that you talk too much?"

She opened her mouth to retort, but Jean-Luc knew her too well.

"Madeleine," he warned, and the vibration of his voice against her sensitive skin made her nearly shoot off the couch.

CHAPTER 7

Madeleine gazed at the water below as it flowed under the bridge. When she'd been here earlier in the day with Chantal, the river had been filled with canoeists, and the streets packed with tourists milling about the market. Now as the sun started to drift off towards the horizon, normality returned to the peaceful village.

The gentle touch of Jean-Luc's fingers, tucking a stray lock of hair behind her ear, drew her attention back to his question.

"Today was quite an education. Chantal really knows her way around the markets we visited, what things are worth, and who would want to buy them."

"An old friend of my father's runs an antiques business. When she showed an interest in interior decorating, I approached Henrique and asked him if he would give her some guidance. I wanted to encourage her without being obvious. If she knew the idea came from me, she would have rebelled."

A couple of teenagers ran onto the bridge, their phones

raised to snap pictures of the spectacular view. Madeleine waited until they moved on before taking a deep breath and turning towards Jean-Luc. This time she would get some answers.

"The garage called earlier about your car."

Another distraction. The man excelled at them.

"Is it bad? Did they say how much it would cost?" The answer filled her with dread. Paying for flights to the Caribbean and forking out more money to come to France had stretched her finances to the limit.

"I believe it's only a small part that needs replacing, but they must place a special order. Your car should be ready tomorrow afternoon."

"But did they say how much the repair would cost?"

He smiled at her indulgently and shrugged. "He mentioned a price, but it doesn't matter. The invoice will go on our account. There is no reason to be concerned."

Annoyance pushed its way to the top of her emotions. First, he deliberately steered the conversation away from the questions he knew she was about to ask, and now he had the audacity to treat her as if she was no different from Chantal. A little girl to be pacified.

Well, he was in for a surprise. She hadn't had a handout from anyone since she left university and had vowed not to take a penny more from her mother. It had been the simplest way to stop her mother from having a hold over her.

"I need to know so I can repay you."

"Don't worry about the invoice. It's nothing. Why don't we relax and enjoy the beautiful evening?" His manner was dismissive, and anger rose inside of Madeleine at his refusal to take her concern seriously.

"Because I'm not someone you're responsible for Jean-

Luc. You can't treat me as if I'm Chantal. You've already been very generous in letting me stay at the chateau, but I can't and I won't let you pay for my car. How much is it going to cost?"

"I don't remember." He turned his gaze back towards the river, his profile stony.

"Jean-Luc, how much is the repair going to cost?"

He turned back to her, exasperation in his eyes. "Mon Dieu. I don't remember. I would have made a note if I thought the issue was important, but he said a figure and it sounded fair to me. There's no need to remember because I trust him to invoice us accordingly. If you like, I can call again tomorrow and ask, but I don't see what difference any of this makes. The car needs fixing. It's at the garage. There's not much that can be done."

"I need to know I can afford the repairs."

"Well, if you can't, it doesn't matter. You can pay me later if it makes you feel better. Now, will you please relax so we can enjoy the evening?"

She huffed but conceded that he was extremely generous in offering to let her repay him when she got home and that she was churlish in not accepting. But damn it, if she let him have his way and accepted everything he offered, she'd be behaving no better than how her mother behaved most of the time.

Jean-Luc sighed and put his arm over her shoulders, drawing her close to him, and kissed her cheek.

"Sorry, chérie. I'm used to handling everything, and no one has ever questioned me before. I insist you pay me back every penny and with interest, too."

"I'd be wiser to pay the garage directly. It will be cheaper." Seeing him flustered and wondering what he needed to say to make it right, Madeleine put him out of his misery. "I'm teasing, Jean-Luc. I'm sorry, too. I guess I'm not used to having someone else fix things for me. Perhaps we're both at fault."

"In that case, I'll take a kiss as a down payment, and we'll say no more about it tonight. Tomorrow I promise I will find out how much the cost will be."

Madeleine was tempted to point out that he was still being patronising when Jean-Luc's hand reached up and turned her face towards him. His lips captured hers in a kiss so quick it was over in a second, but long enough for her to forget about being annoyed.

"Come on, let's walk." He took her hand and helped her down some steps that led to a path by the river. The water lapped against the bank, its colour now a dark orange as the sun disappeared behind the buildings in the town. They walked in uncomfortable silence for a few moments. Madeleine needed him to answer her questions, but the closer she got to asking them, the less sure she was that she wanted to hear the answers.

"What are Chantal's nightmares about? Is it to do with your mother's death?"

"Yes." He spoke so softly she had to strain to hear him, despite the stillness of the evening.

"My mother's death was not an accident. My stepfather killed her before taking his own life."

A cold chill crept down Madeleine's back.

"We believe Chantal saw everything." Jean-Luc paused for a moment as if unsure how to continue. He took a depth breath, let it out slowly, and then started to walk again.

"Their marriage had always been volatile. They loved each other, but jealousy, misunderstandings, and distrust caused many arguments. Eventually their relationship spiralled out of control. The rows became worse when Chantal was about nine, fuelled by my stepfather's drinking."

Her throat contracted as she imagined the life for that little girl.

"I was away a lot at the time. I was angry with my mother, my stepfather, and the rest of the world in general. As soon as I was old enough, I left the chateau, only returning occasionally."

Jean-Luc ran a hand though his hair, clearly disturbed by the memories flooding back. He stared straight ahead across the river into the darkness as night fell. Madeleine felt the pain radiating off him. She held her breath, waiting, dreading his next words.

"Danielle found the three of them in my mother's studio. She said there was chaos and blood everywhere, and in the middle of it all was Chantal, as still as a statue, staring into oblivion."

Madeleine stopped walking, stunned at what he'd said. The abrupt halt of their movement made him pull on her hand, and he swung back towards her. Her emotions wavered between horror for what Chantal had been through and compassion for the man in front of her left to pick up the pieces.

"Was she hurt?"

"No. There was some bruising and minor cuts, but she had fallen into a state of shock. She just stared into space for days afterwards. Danielle couldn't contact me. I'd gone off with Raph somewhere. She was so concerned for her that she put Chantal into a private hospital."

No wonder no one used the studio now. Madeleine would have left the chateau for good.

"That's the part I find the hardest to deal with, that I wasn't there for her." A hoarseness in his voice gave away the depth of his emotion. "My mother and stepfather were already on the road to self-destruction. I don't believe I could have made a difference, but I should never have left Chantal alone with them."

The weight of his pain caused a wave of sympathy to wash over Madeleine for the young man who must have been so confused after losing so much. She reached up and held his cheek in her palm.

"You were what, eighteen?"

"Twenty." He turned back around and started walking again. Still holding tightly onto his hand, Madeleine fell into step beside him.

"You were young. You can't blame yourself for the way your parents behaved."

"But I do hold myself responsible for not being around when she needed me. It took Danielle nearly a week to track me down." His tone said how disgusted he was with himself. The sorrow cut straight to Madeleine's heart that she could do nothing to relieve him of the notion that someone so young should be accountable for the way others lead their lives.

"So does Chantal remember anything?"

"She says not, only a fight beforehand, but sometimes I wonder if snippets haven't returned."

He paused and stared directly into Madeleine's eyes, his expression inscrutable. She couldn't break his gaze, and the invisible hold he had on her, even if she'd wanted to. He reached out and distractedly ran her hair through his fingertips, and Madeleine felt an inexplicable pleasure in the solace the simple gesture seemed to give him.

"Occasionally she looks at me as if she wants to say something, but can't. I probably don't make the discussion any easier for her. I'm not only her brother but also the one who still scolds her, too."

They continued to walk again.

"Like the Paris excursion?"

He gave her a cautious glance.

"Chantal mentioned today you weren't impressed with her last shopping expedition."

"Exactly. One minute she's all adult and in control, the next she's behaving like a spoilt brat."

"Hmm, sounds like she and my mother would get along perfectly." Madeleine tried to inject a little humour back into the conversation.

"The trouble is I think I'm the reason she's like that."

Madeleine started to reiterate her earlier thoughts, but Jean-Luc interrupted her.

"No. I mean that I indulge her. When the shock wore off and the nightmares began, I would do anything to ease her pain. I found myself unable to say no to her requests, however unreasonable they were. By the time I wised up that perhaps giving into her wasn't the right tack, it was too late." A philosophical smile fleetingly crossed his face. "I'd created a monster."

"Actually, illicit excursions aside, I'd say you've done a great job. You should have seen her today in the market. She's a force to be reckoned with." Sensing his reticence to believe her, Madeleine drove her point home. "Seriously, Jean-Luc, I couldn't help but admire her."

He sat on a bench next to the water and pulled her down

to sit with him. His tone dropped low again, his voice almost a whisper. "I can't see it. I just see the scared, frightened little girl she was then." Madeleine gazed into Jean-Luc's eyes. She saw them glistening with unshed tears for his sister, and her heart cracked a little. "Weeks went by before she would even talk about what happened. I don't ever want her to go through the pain again. Keeping her close is my way of protecting her."

"Do you not think maybe a little freedom might do her good?"

His face hardened. "It's a case of knowing who to trust. Their deaths were big news when it happened. People we thought were our friends sold their story without a second thought to how the scandal would affect Chantal. She doesn't remember the details. I worry one day the whole thing will come crashing forward in her mind, and I won't be there to support her." He gave her a wry smile. "Chantal, obviously, doesn't feel the same way."

"Were you always close?"

"Yes. Despite our age difference, our difficult home life brought us together. By the time Chantal was about eight, the problems were becoming increasingly apparent. I just wanted to ignore them." His voice drifted off.

"But you can't ignore an eight-year-old."

"No. I couldn't leave her in the house with them fighting, so on those days I used to take her out with me and Raph. Although the way we teased her, I don't know whether she thought it was better. But several months later, I had a big argument with my stepfather and left."

Madeleine sensed the conversation was about to go full circle. She took a chance that she wouldn't make him angry and ventured quietly, "You can't spend your life berating yourself for something you didn't know was going to happen. You must move forward one day."

He said nothing, but an owl somewhere in the darkness hooted its agreement. They sat in silence for a while, both lost in their own thoughts, their hands intertwined.

"Is there a dungeon at the chateau?"

"No. Why?" At his startled expression, Madeleine smiled.

"I thought it would go well with my image yesterday when I woke up to the sound of screams in the night."

Picking up on Madeleine's unspoken suggestion to end the evening on a lighter note, Jean-Luc leaned over and kissed the back of her neck. A warm shiver ran down her spine as he said in a low voice, "I can think of better ways to torture you than in a cold, damp dungeon."

LATER THAT NIGHT, WHEN THEY RETURNED TO THE CHATEAU, Jean-Luc led Madeleine to his room. The man filled with regret and uncertainty earlier had been left behind in the shadows of the night. Now Jean-Luc was back to his normal, commanding self, and for once Madeleine was happy to give up control and be swept along by the night's emotions.

The moment the bedroom door shut, his lips were on hers, his hands everywhere at once, removing her clothes, caressing her body, fuelling the ecstasy he'd started back beside the river until Madeleine couldn't think straight. Not waiting to make it to the bed, Jean-Luc lifted her legs around him and thrust himself deep within her, pressing her back against the closed door. Madeleine came with a speed that surprised her, and Jean-Luc followed almost immediately. They clung to each other in the aftermath, panting, sweat dripping from their bodies, but their minds released from the recollections of the night.

Madeleine didn't know how long they stood together, but eventually Jean-Luc picked her up and placed her under the soothing spray of a hot shower. This time they took things slowly, discovering how to drive each other to the brink of madness, only to pull back and start all over again. By the time they fell into bed, Madeleine could barely keep her eyes open, but she still needed to ask Jean-Luc one more question.

"Why did you stay at the chateau?"

"It's my home. Regardless of what happened, there are a lot of good memories here that don't deserve to be forgotten." He looked deep into her eyes and kissed her gently, his lips melting against hers. "And I hope many new ones to make, too."

CHAPTER 8

Morning sunlight filtered through the shutters and into Jean-Luc's consciousness. On a normal day, he would be up and getting ready, but for now he was content to remain where he was, with Madeleine's warm body curled snugly into his.

Rarely did anyone stay at the house with him. When Chantal was younger, he didn't want to disrupt her routine. Now it was an easy way to keep relationships compartmentalised. He never promised his dates anything more than a good time, and not bringing women back to the chateau stopped things from getting complicated.

He used his apartment near the factory sometimes, but that was different. The chateau was his private life, one he guarded closely. Of course, women still constantly vied for an invite, but he managed to avoid requests without too much confrontation. If they couldn't take no for an answer, then he moved on.

He pushed himself up on the pillow and looked down at the woman beside him. Her hair mussed from his fingers, she seemed every bit the sprite he'd called her when they'd first met.

There was something different about Madeleine, a softness which made him want to explore both her mind and her body. More surprisingly, he wanted her to understand him, too. He never talked to anybody except his close friends about his mother and Chantal. Last night when he'd told her, an inexplicable sense of relief had washed over him.

The lack of pity in her eyes drew him to her. With Madeleine's compassion and understanding of the blame he placed upon himself, he found a strength within which had evaded him until now. A courage to perhaps make some changes for the better. No one had ever made him feel that way before.

Madeleine's eyes opened, mesmerising him once again with their intense greenness.

"Salut, chérie." He claimed her soft lips with the kiss he'd wanted since waking.

"Hi." Her mouth tilted up in a shy smile, but the shrill sound of a mobile phone stopped him short of his next move. Madeleine sighed. "My mother. I need to answer it." She scrambled out of bed and reached for the top she'd worn the night before.

"Hi, Mum." She cradled the phone in her neck as she tried to button up her blouse. He smiled at Madeleine's sharp intake of breath when he came behind her and took over from her fingers, taking the opportunity to press his naked form into her back.

As Madeleine tensed up, Jean-Luc couldn't resist teasing her some more and lowered his head to kiss the pale skin of her neck, tantalisingly revealed as she switched the phone from one ear to the other. He heard the muffled sound of her mother talking.

"Yes, I'm still staying with my friend." She shrugged off his embrace and turned around. Her eyes blazed like emerald daggers, silently telling him to back off. He raised his hands, feigning innocence, but took the hint and went into the bathroom, giving the illusion of allowing Madeleine to continue her conversation in private.

Jean-Luc left the door open so he could listen. He wanted to know more about her wayward mother and deceitful boyfriend. He'd learnt during Chantal's teenage years it was simpler to overhear something and figure out the rest than to ask what was going on. And Madeleine was definitely pricklier than a teenager, especially when it came to her mother.

While brushing his teeth, he listened to Madeleine explaining about her car.

"I told you it's being fixed. Just a couple more days and then I will be with you, but you're okay, aren't you?" Despite her previous protestations to the contrary, Jean-Luc heard the concern in her voice.

"Are you sure?" He stared at Madeleine in the reflection of the bathroom mirror. An expression of agitation marred her face. "So, is that why you went there?" Her tone took on a hint of accusation. "I understand, Mum, but that's not what I asked. Just exactly who is with you?"

She paced around the room, one hand holding the phone, the other one running over her forehead and through her hair. "Relax, Mum. You're probably just overreacting. I'll be there soon, and we can study everything together. I've already got some information from someone at work, so perhaps we'll have a head start."

She did? News to him. What did she find out? All she'd

told him was the guy stole some money. If Madeleine had discovered more than that, it must mean it wasn't the first time the asshole had pulled this stunt, which probably meant he was already known to the police. Jean-Luc shook his head in disbelief. Now she was chasing him down, thanks to her foolish mother.

He slammed down the toothbrush. He was one step behind, and it didn't bode well. Madeleine glanced up, and their eyes clashed in the mirror. Taking the hint, he pushed the door to and continued getting ready.

He wanted to understand more about the situation, but asking Madeleine would be futile. She was edgy enough about the car being mended. No way would she volunteer anything if she thought he would interfere.

But he couldn't leave it alone. He'd done that once before and look what had happened.

He caught his reflection in the shower door and stood still for a moment. When had she slipped past his guard and into his protection? Until now, he hadn't thought about how much he liked the way she saw the hidden talents within Chantal or, regardless of how mad she was with her mother, the way she was still concerned. And perhaps, the sweetest of all, the way she made him stronger by not judging him as harshly as he did himself.

Alors, maybe it had crossed his mind, but he'd never met anyone like Madeleine before. From the moment he first saw her, she'd intrigued him. The more he discovered about her, the more he wanted to know.

If Madeleine was going to leave the chateau and follow her mother to the South of France, he needed to find out what she was going to face and create a plan that included him going with her.

Time to take a different tack. In an instant it came to him. There was no one better than Chantal for digging out information without raising suspicion. He'd enlist her help and get her to relay what she discovered later. Satisfied with his plan, he stepped into the shower, ignoring the voice telling him he'd never gone to this much trouble for a woman before.

"Is everything okay?" Jean-Luc asked as he sauntered back into the room.

She'd gone back to bed after finishing her phone call. He watched as Madeleine's gaze was drawn to his fingers buttoning up his shirt and then dropped lower to his stomach. His mind filled with images of her exploring every inch of it a few hours before. His hands stilled, and her green eyes swept upwards, mirroring the desire building inside him.

"Keep looking at me like that and I may never get to the office today." He walked over to give her a long, lingering kiss before straightening up to finish dressing. Temptation that didn't sit well in his rigorously controlled life swept over him, and Jean-Luc steeled himself against listening to his body.

"It's okay. I promised Chantal a game of tennis this morning."

"How easily I'm forgotten." He feigned wounded pride. "As much as I'd like to stay, I must go." With more abruptness than he'd intended, Jean-Luc gave Madeleine a perfunctory kiss, straightened up, and slipped on his jacket.

He glanced back at her as he opened the bedroom door, and his body grew hard at the picture she made. The covers twisted around her body, barely covering her breasts, her unconscious allure reeling him in. He needed to leave before he drowned, gladly, in the madness.

"A tout à l'heure."

Before Madeleine could respond, he shut the door.

As she sat in the kitchen eating breakfast by herself, Madeleine mulled over how she seriously needed to get a grip back on her life. It was all very well living in some romantic holiday fantasy, but at some point reality would come crashing down. There was no way she was going to be the one left standing there alone while an enigmatic Frenchman rode off into the sunset without her. Everlasting love only existed in the movies. The sooner she met up with her mother and sorted out her problems, the faster she could get back home to the normality of her life in London.

After speaking to her mother this morning, Madeleine had the distinct feeling she hadn't been told everything. It was unusual for her mother to hold back, and it left Madeleine uneasy. Her mother might manipulate the truth in order to get her own way, but keeping information to herself wasn't her style. She played out every drama, no matter how small, to the fullest.

Normally, the solution to her mother's problems would simply appear after some thought, but this time, it was proving impossible. Until the pair of them figured out where Jackson was, they didn't stand a chance in hell of persuading him to give the money back. Her mother had said that while the police were sympathetic, there was little they could do. Jeff, in his email, said to follow where the wealthy people go because Jackson would want to score again, which was certainly the South of France. Maybe her mother concluded the same thing.

Jean-Luc clouded her thoughts. He'd being doing that a

lot lately. She huffed out a sigh. Why didn't he understand there was a reason some things had an expiry date? Many years ago, she'd vowed she wasn't going to be the little girl back at boarding school again, hoping against hope that her mother would miss her as much as she did. It was better to never know what you might miss than to try and survive the disappointment.

Yesterday, when Jean-Luc had showed her around his business, it confirmed what she already recognised deep down. Here was a man who took care of everyone under his protection. He never let anyone down. He simply wouldn't allow it. She couldn't begin to imagine what it must have been like to lose his mother, be left with a frightened child to care for and start a business. If she stayed here much longer, he'd take her under his wing, too, and she didn't want to be a burden, someone he helped out from a sense of duty. It would be at odds with the passion they'd shared, and he'd grow to resent her. She'd seen it too many times with her mother.

She needed to take charge of her life again, and the first thing to do was get her car back. Finishing off her piece of toast and draining the last of her coffee, Madeleine rose determinedly and went off to find Chantal.

MADELEINE LOOKED ACROSS THE CAR AND FROWNED. Chantal's concentration wasn't on her driving. With the window wound down, her arm waving about in the hot afternoon sun, she should surely be steering a peddle boat, not a car. But Madeleine was too pleased to be fetching her own vehicle to worry about asking Chantal to put both hands on the wheel.

After persuading Chantal to ring the garage to check if her car was ready for collection, she tried to get hold of her mother on the phone without success. Inevitably, it became the subject of conversation on the way to the garage.

"Charles Jackson? But that's the point. He was so charming. All my mother's friends adored him."

"Just how much did they like him?" Chantal glanced over, her delicately plucked eyebrows raised, emphasising the meaning of her words.

"Oh." Dread washed over Madeleine. The beauty of the bright summer's day diminished as the full weight of the realisation hit her. "I didn't even think of that. Do you think he persuaded others to invest as well?"

"I don't know how much money your mother put in, but he's not going to make a killing with only one investor, is he?"

Madeleine recognised Chantal's assessment of the situation was probably spot on. Other pieces of conversation with her mother began to slip into place, and a picture started to form.

"Now it's all starting to make sense. She's gone down to the south with Gene because he's invested, too. I'm such an idiot. Why didn't I see it before? I thought the other investors would be strangers to my mother."

"Presumably they didn't choose the south on a whim?"

"No." Madeleine knew instinctively Chantal was right with her assumption. Her mother must have figured something else out and hadn't bothered to tell her. "Shit. I've got to get going and hope I'm not too late."

Madeleine fought down the worry that consumed her for the remainder of the short trip into the village. She was jolted back to reality when Chantal drove into the forecourt of the garage and stopped the car by pulling the handbrake up hard. Who on earth had taught her to drive? She turned to ask, but the words died on her lips when she saw concern in the other woman's eyes.

Chantal grabbed Madeleine's forearm and leaned across the seat. "You know he never brings anyone home, don't you?"

"Who, Charles?" She'd never heard Chantal talk so seriously before, and it puzzled her for a moment.

Chantal gaped at her as if she was stupid.

"Jean-Luc, of course!"

Madeleine thought back to the first day they met on the road and smiled at the memory. "But he didn't bring me home, not like you mean. He was being kind and helping me out."

"Non. You don't understand, do you? Helping you out would be giving you a lift to the hotel in the village. He brought you home." She placed great emphasis on the last word. "Just think about it, that's all I'm saying."

With that, she got out of the car, leaving Madeleine feeling slightly disoriented.

CHAPTER 9

Jean-Luc was finishing up a meeting when Chantal's call came through. He didn't focus on what she was saying immediately, but when the implications sank in, his gut tightened.

"Chantal, you're talking too fast. Start again at the beginning." He thought Madeleine would be on her way soon, but he'd hoped they'd have a few more days together so he could figure out what to do next.

"Madeleine made me take her to fetch her car. I knew you'd be mad, but don't blame me. She's as forceful as you once she gets started. On the way there, she realised that her mother must know where…" She paused.

"Jackson?" Jean-Luc interjected, almost spitting out the word. He'd already found out more than enough about him during the morning.

"Yes, Jackson. She realises he's down in the south and maybe her mother's friend has lost money, too, and that's why he's with her."

Jean-Luc had come to the same conclusion earlier. It was

unlikely Madeleine's mother would be the only investor trying to hunt him down.

"You need to come home, Jean-Luc. I'm sure she'll start packing as soon as she gets back to the chateau. She seemed pretty upset that she'd not thought of it before."

"Where are you now?" He shrugged into his jacket and grabbed his car keys.

"We're just leaving the garage. I'll follow her home."

"I suppose she's paid the bill?"

"What do you think? I tried to insist the invoice could go on our account, but that's not her style, is it?"

A frown crossed his face. No, it wasn't. Independent to the end, that was Madeleine. No reliance on anyone but herself, even if it was to her detriment. He'd admire her for her determination if it didn't drive him crazy.

"I'm leaving now." He was already half-way across the carpark. "Whatever you do, do not let her leave before I get back."

Cursing that the drive from the factory to the chateau was taking longer than normal because of tourist traffic, Jean-Luc mulled over what his security contractor had dug up on Charles Jackson. The guy was wanted in both Australia and the UK for fraud and from what he understood was currently working his way across Europe.

Unlike some fraudsters who were merely slick talkers, this guy's reputation included using force when things didn't go his way. In his opinion, Madeleine's mother was lucky he'd done a disappearing act. She'd do better to leave the entire mess to the authorities than to try to find him. However, since that wasn't an option, he needed another plan, and fast. He hit the favourites tab on the call screen and phoned ahead to make arrangements.

Twenty minutes later, he all but skidded to a halt in the courtyard, having torn up the gravel as he came down the driveway at breakneck speed. Ignoring Danielle's flustered and confused expression as she opened the front door, he took the stairs two at a time.

When he reached the open door of the bedroom, his heart sank at the sight of Madeleine gathering up the last few items into her handbag, her case packed beside the bed like she couldn't wait to leave. Annoyance, anger, and a disappointment he didn't want to analyse rose within him.

"WERE YOU GOING TO WAIT FOR ME TO RETURN?"

Madeleine spun round. Jean-Luc had taken her by surprise, but she wasn't fooled by his calm, silky voice and casual pose against the door jamb or the dark, dangerous glint of challenge in his eyes.

"Yes, of course." Her hands shook as she tried to close the leather clasp. Silently cursing their betrayal of her emotional state, Madeleine summoned up every piece of strength she had to continue in a steady voice. "Chantal said you were returning straight away." Now she sounded as if she was obeying his orders. A slither of defiance she desperately needed filled her with courage. "Besides, I'm still waiting for my mother to return my call."

"You're packed, though, n'est-ce pas?" His unspoken question of whether she'd still be there if her mother had called was clear by the tone of his voice.

She chose to ignore it.

"Talking to Chantal, the pieces fell into place. I'm certain I'm right. Mum has followed Charles down there, so she must know more than she's let on."

He stood still and didn't say a word. The heat from his stare caused her neck to itch.

"He must be there, and that explains why she's gone, too. It's the only thing that makes sense." Even to her own ears, she sounded nervous. Sitting on the chair beside the dressing table, Madeleine bent down as if to check for something in her bag. She couldn't meet Jean-Luc's gaze. He'd recognise the hesitation and uncertainty in her eyes straight away. "I'm packed because I want to be able to go immediately, if I'm right."

"To the South of France?"

"Yes. Jeff said Charles would be wherever the money is, and I can't think of anywhere more likely in France."

"And who the hell is Jeff?" The force of his tone took Madeleine by surprise. She lifted her head up sharply. Jean-Luc was no longer by the door, but standing over her. Anger radiated off him. He leaned in and placed his hands on either side of the chair she was sitting on.

"Who is he, Madeleine? Someone else you did your little lost girl act on to convince them to come to your rescue?"

"What? How dare you!" The unjustified attack stung. Not to mention he'd made her out to be as bad as her mother. "You think I stood at the side of the road waiting for you to come by and fix my car? Oh, and by the way, my mother's having a bit of a problem, do you think you could help with that, too? Get real!"

Frustrated, Madeleine jumped to her feet to force Jean-Luc to take a few steps backwards and give her space to think. Time to regain control of her emotions. Did he think so little of her? A hard lump formed in her throat. Maybe it was just as well she was leaving.

She lifted her head and met Jean-Luc's steady gaze. "He's

a guy from work in the fraud department whom I cajoled into seeing if he could find out any more about Charles Jackson."

Or did that make her the same as her mother after all?

Jean-Luc took a deep breath and ran his hands through his hair. "Sorry. There's no excuse, except sometimes I can't think straight around you."

She knew that feeling well.

"What did this Jeff discover?" His emphasis on her friend's name rankled.

"Nothing. All he could find is some trace of him a few years ago in Australia, but then the trail goes dead."

A flash of recognition crossed Jean-Luc's eyes, but it vanished again in an instant. His face returned to its normal dark, unfathomable expression.

"I'm coming with you." His tone said he'd take no argument, but Madeleine was ready for one.

"Don't be ridiculous. It's my problem to sort out. After all, you can't up and leave everything just to keep an eye on a lost girl," she threw back at him.

"Why not?" Arms folded across his chest, he waited for her answer. His eyes bored into hers, and Madeleine worried about how much he saw there.

Because I'm not and don't want to be your responsibility. Because we need to end this before I'm in too deep. Because the amazing things we've shared will get lost in a daze of bitterness and hatred when this inevitably doesn't work out. She shouted the words so loudly in her head he could surely hear them, but the silence in the room while he waited for her to answer was deafening.

She cleared her throat. "Because you have enough to worry about here with Chantal." Her voice was much calmer than she felt. "Anyway, as you've pointed out, we've only just met. You don't even know my mother."

"We might have just met, as you so quaintly put it." Jean-Luc's sarcastic tone almost made Madeleine wince. "But I'd hoped with what we'd shared you would at least place me on a little higher standing. Of course I'm coming with you."

His exasperation with her only made her dig her heels in further.

"Holiday flings are supposed to be just a short spell of self-indulgence. Simple, uncomplicated, remembered fondly."

Jean-Luc scoffed at the *fondly*. "Except it isn't simple, is it, Madeleine?" She held her breath, wondering what he might say next. "In your head you'd like it to be, but in your heart, I think it's different."

"You keep telling yourself that, chéri." She bit in with her own cynicism, using the emotion to push away any wavering her heart might be considering. "In the meantime, I've got my car back and I need to get on."

"As easy as that?" He moved closer, his hand stroking gently down her spine, causing a spark of electricity to jolt through her. "What about the passion?" His voice lowered seductively. "The connection we share. You can't deny you don't feel it here." He covered his own heart with his hand.

Madeleine struggled to portray indifference. "It's just an emotion that clouds judgement and sanity."

"You said it." Frustration crept into his tone. "I must be insane for trying to talk you into letting me come with you."

A twinge of annoyance brooded within Madeleine. He still considered her a responsibility. "You more than anyone should understand. It's not as if you can look back on a perfect family relationship and believe in happily ever after."

"Merde." Jean-Luc's hands rose up angrily beside her, and he stepped away, putting distance between them. "You never give up. Of course I understand, but I can recognise the difference between self-destructive relationships and those that make you feel alive. The only reason your mother doesn't grow up and take responsibility for her own life is because you don't give her the chance."

"Oh, that's rich coming from the man who's like the Spanish inquisition every time Chantal wants to do something."

She'd pushed him too far. She could see it in his eyes as he strode back across the room.

His jaw clenched as his face loomed in front of hers, his voice dangerously calm. "So you're not jeopardising your nice, safe life because emotions are messy? Well, it's about to get a whole lot dirtier, chérie."

His assault on her lips surprised her. Swept along by a desire that refused to be battened down, Madeleine responded with the same force he gave. The power struggle moved from words to actions, but each one of them gave as much as they took. When Jean-Luc's hands twisted themselves in her hair, pulling her lips even closer, and his tongue invaded her mouth in a hostile takeover of her senses, Madeleine fought back with her own offence. Her determination to stay in control brought their kiss to a fevered pitch.

HE KNEW THIS WASN'T THE WAY TO WIN A BATTLE WITH Madeleine, but she drove him to the edge. He wanted to strangle her or kiss her, and the latter held so much more appeal. He wanted to shake her out of the fortress she hid behind. To excite and inflame her as much as she did him.

Slowly fury gave way to gentler, more seductive kisses, and Jean-Luc lost himself to the spell Madeleine always seemed to cast over him. His hands drifting down her body brought back the memory of the jealousy that had ripped through him earlier at the mention of another man's name. He'd taken his displeasure out on Madeleine, but it was himself he was angry with. Where had such a powerful emotion come from? And how was he going to be able to control it when Madeleine left for England, as she was sure to do?

The thought made him reluctantly break off the kiss. There was so much still to be resolved between them, and he needed to think clearly. He looked down at her suitcases.

"I need to pack." Walking over to the wall, he ran his fingers along the underneath of a ridge of panelling, searching for the clasp. The hidden door swung open as he released the catch, and he heard Madeleine gasp. A grim smile crossed his lips. For a change, she was speechless.

Bien. He needed to defuse their argument if he was going to get his way.

He walked through to his bedroom. By the time Madeleine followed him, he'd already put a couple of shirts into a small travel case.

"These used to be my parents' rooms. I think my mother was always disappointed the chateau didn't have any secret chambers, so she had the door installed shortly before my father's death. Look at the door from this side of the room. It's a little more obvious."

He watched as she studied the door from both sides. In her room the opening was completely disguised by the panelling, but in his it was given away by the gaps in the wallpaper outlining the shape of the door offset by the discreet handle halfway down.

"Did your parents have separate rooms?"

Jean-Luc wasn't fooled. From the pointed way she glared at his case he knew Madeleine hadn't given up on their argument. This was only a reprieve.

"No, Maman planned on using your room as a nursery."

"She didn't use it when Chantal was born?"

"She didn't use either of these rooms when she remarried."

"Too many memories." Her voice was so soft it was as if she didn't mean to say the words out loud.

He shrugged. "I started using them after her death. It was closer to Chantal—as you know, she is across the hall—and this has always been my favourite outlook from the chateau."

"The fields you and Raphael ran through as boys, no cares, no responsibilities, just the magic of the countryside."

"Précisément."

He walked across the room and took her face in his hands, kissing her forehead.

"There are few people who see me as I am. Mostly to people I am Chantal's brother, someone's employer, a colleague, a rich man to buy gifts, a knight to rescue a la naïade." He couldn't stop his lips from tilting into a small smile as he teased her. "Then you say something, and I realise you see right through the confusion of my life to the man I am." He broke away, knowing that he was getting distracted again.

Madeleine stared at the connecting door.

"So when Danielle showed me to my room, was it

because she usually..." The sentence trailed off, but Jean-Luc understood what Madeleine was asking. Did he often bring women home? How little did she realise.

"She did so at my request."

When her mobile rang, Jean-Luc ignored Madeleine's protests and picked up the phone.

"Bonjour, Madame Smythe, this is Jean-Luc Delacroix... oui, Madeleine's friend... she is... no, I didn't know that."

Madeleine rolled her eyes. "Give me the phone back. There's no time for chitchat." She grasped for the phone, but Jean-Luc used his height advantage to keep it out of reach.

"Madame Smythe... Barbara."

Madeleine groaned and shook her head, but Jean-Luc ignored her and continued his conversation.

"While it's great to speak with you at last, I need to ask you a few questions about Charles Jackson... yes, Madeleine mentioned something about him. Have you seen him?... but you didn't approach, ah bien... No, no, whatever you do, do not try to make contact. Madeleine and I will arrive in a couple of hours, and we can discuss it over drinks... text the Nice address to Madeleine's phone... oui, oui... à bientôt."

By the time he'd finished the call, Madeleine didn't know whether to carry on being annoyed with his high-handedness or laugh at his lack of understanding of the finer details.

"Tell me, if I let you come with me, how are we going to do five hundred miles in two hours?"

"It's not so far if you travel direct." Madeleine detected a hint of smugness in Jean-Luc's voice.

"Seriously?"

"Bien sûr, of course. It's too dangerous for you to go by yourself, so you're coming with me." The distant sound of a helicopter approaching filled the silent pause. "Your chariot awaits."

Madeleine knew when she was outmanoeuvred and resigned herself to the inevitable. "Okay, we'll go together, but Jean-Luc, remember, this is only a holiday romance."

He regarded her nonchalantly. "If you're not having a good time, perhaps you need a little reminding?"

"Don't get me wrong, I've had a fabulous time, but nothing ever lasts forever, not in my experience, so there's no point dragging it out to its inevitable conclusion. When the holiday's over, so are we."

She wasn't sure if the extra emphasis on the words were to remind herself or to convince him.

He kissed her firmly on the lips as he bent down to pick up her bags. "Then let's enjoy it for the moment, chérie."

But the warmth of his kiss didn't quite reach his eyes, and as the air between them chilled, she wondered why she felt just a little bereft.

CHAPTER 10

I f she hadn't been so tense, Madeleine would have enjoyed looking down at the patchwork of fields and forests passing rapidly below them. Villages dissected by rivers, lakes glinting in the sunlight, church spires rising above ancient rooftops. Instead, she tapped her fingers against the armrest. Distracted by both Jean-Luc sitting beside her and concerned that her mother would do something stupid, she thought about the events of the last few hours.

The day started brightly enough, but despite the blue skies surrounding them, she could feel a storm brewing between her and Jean-Luc. He accused her of leading a safe life, but he didn't understand how much not doing so had cost her in the past. Life was simpler if she didn't get emotionally involved.

Lost in thought, her eyes began to close, and she relaxed into the oblivion that sleep brought.

A thought broke into Madeleine's consciousness as the helicopter raced through the French countryside. She'd told

Jean-Luc a bit about her mother's dilemma, but nothing specific.

The notion nagged at her, finally bringing her awake, only to be disoriented by the closeness of Jean-Luc. The scent of him engulfed her, assailing her senses and sending a shiver of awareness down her spine. Her head rested on his shoulder. While she wanted nothing more than to savour the illicit feeling running through her, there was a pressing question that needed to be answered.

"How do you know he's dangerous?"

She thought back through their conversations over the last few days and couldn't recall giving any detailed information, with good reason. For one thing, he would insist on getting involved, but also she wanted to stop real life from intruding on her fantasy holiday romance. Apparently she'd been deluded on both fronts.

Shaking herself awake, she sat up straighter, trying to clear her jumbled thoughts.

Until she'd read Jeff's email, she'd known nothing about Charles Jackson apart from what she'd gleaned from her mother over the last ten months. So why did Jean-Luc describe Charles as a threat?

Jean-Luc gave her a wary glance that could only be interpreted as busted. Not a hint of guilt, she noted, and judging by the way he shifted uncomfortably in his seat, he sensed he was in for another argument, which meant he thought she'd guessed already. She thought about it for a moment, and then leaned over the armrest separating their seats to make sure he heard every word, even though they were wearing headsets.

"Chantal. She wasn't just chatting over a game of tennis this morning, was she?"

Jean-Luc shrugged in response, not meeting her gaze. The thrum of the helicopter blades filled the silence, vibrating through Madeleine's brain as she tried to make sense of it.

Annoyance and anger rose up easily within her after their previous argument a short while ago. To think he claimed she avoided complicated situations.

"So you use your sister without a second thought to interfere with someone else's life, but you don't think she's responsible enough to make decisions on her own." She threw herself back into the seat, venting her own frustrations at being manipulated.

His black gaze pinned her there as he swung his head around. His deep voice filled her headset as he spoke to the pilot. A curt affirmation to Jean-Luc's command, followed by the flicking of a switch in the cockpit, made Madeleine realise that their conversation had not been private.

"Charles Jackson isn't just some small time con-artist."

He'd neatly avoided her question. There was no other possible explanation other than Chantal. Why hadn't he just asked her? *Because you wouldn't have told him.*

"He's wanted for questioning on at least two continents by both the police and several financial institutions. Not only for fraud, but maybe murder, too. I suspect one of the appeals of your mother, besides her money, is that her house offered him somewhere quiet to lie low for a while."

Madeleine fell silent for a few moments. Confusion and shock replaced anger. How did he know so much more than her in such a short space of time?

"But he moved in with Mum nearly a year ago. If he's as ruthless as you make him out to be, wouldn't he have gone elsewhere before now?" She didn't doubt the authenticity of his information, but she needed to understand.

"Not if he's playing the long game. It takes more than a few months for banks to stop looking for the kind of money he's been creaming off them."

As the helicopter banked around to the east, heading towards Nice, Jean-Luc continued to explain how her mother's latest Mr. Right was wanted for questioning in relation to a fatal fire, extortion, and fraud. That staying with her mother meant he didn't need to rely on his own money, making the cash harder to trace when he did start using it.

Madeleine's heart sank as she realised that this time her mother had made a serious error in judgement. She'd not only put her faith and trust in someone, but her savings and possibly her own life as well.

"How did you find out so much information, so fast?" The fight went out of her. Now she just wanted to get to Nice as quickly as possible.

"Being reliant on global suppliers for the success of the company, it pays to know all about our partners. We use the services of one of the best security companies in the business. I'm not sure I want the details of how they find out, but anything I want to know never takes long." He shrugged at seeing the question in her eyes. "They've always been accurate before."

He reached over and held her hand, giving it a gentle squeeze. At the sudden warmth, Madeleine realised a cold wave of fear had taken hold as the implications of Jean-Luc's words started to sink in.

"Did you ever meet him?" He probed gently.

"No. I've not seen Mum for about eighteen months, not since Bora Bora." Silence filled the cabin for a moment.

"I hear it's beautiful there."

He was waiting for her to add a little detail, but she was too concerned about the now to be distracted by her mother's past antics.

"It is."

He gave her a quizzical look.

"You don't want to know."

He tilted his head and stared at her with impatience. She shrugged and removed her hand from his, crossing her arms.

"Another man, another place."

"Exactly how many times has your mother needed rescuing?" Judging by the incredulous inflection in his voice, he was finally starting to comprehend that she hadn't been exaggerating about how often her mother relied on her for intervening when life got tough.

"I don't know, I've lost count." She turned to stare out the window of the helicopter. The coastline was gradually coming into view. "You do the math. Eighteen months is about average for a relationship. Her record is three years."

"And you accuse me of not relinquishing control of my family."

She glanced at him. Humour and self-depreciation reflected back in his eyes. He was mocking both of them.

"It's not about control. It's a guilt complex, and she gets me every time. Anyway, don't think you can distract me." She poked his arm with her finger. "I haven't forgotten about Chantal."

He grasped her hand and pulled it across his waist, drawing her to him and kissing her swiftly.

"You have to hand it to her, though." A smirk crossed his lips. "She'd make a great spy."

Madeleine laughed and kissed him back. "You are an impossible man."

As Nice appeared in the distance, Jean-Luc grew serious again.

"Madeleine, I'm not sure what you intended to do, but when we arrive, I'm going to insist your mother leave and hand everything over to the authorities."

"To be honest, I don't know what to do next. Normally I turn up, we talk the problem through, and a plan seems to materialise." There was no point in denying it. After Jean-Luc divulged his information about Charles Jackson, she was undoubtedly out of her depth.

"That's not going to happen this time. The only plan is to tell the police and leave. It's too dangerous for her, and that puts you in the line of fire. While she might be prepared to risk your life, I'm not." For once, Madeleine didn't argue.

By the time they arrived at the airport in Nice, Madeleine was so nervous she virtually leapt out of the helicopter. What was up with her? She'd rescued her mother from more dangerous locations than one of the playground areas for the rich and famous. It seemed ludicrous to be so stressed. Even if Jackson turned out to be a murderer, she had no intentions of getting that close to him in the first place.

The man sitting beside her in the taxi didn't help matters. Every time she went near Jean-Luc, her pulse skyrocketed and a blush crept up her cheeks. It wasn't an image she wanted her mother seeing because she'd instantly put the wrong meaning on it. But looking at his stony profile next to her, she knew ditching him while she met with her mother alone wasn't going to be an option.

Back at the chateau, she'd planned exactly what she was going to say. Experience taught her it was always easier to end a relationship before it got too serious. Life was simpler, less complicated that way, and far less prone to disappointment. So why was Jean-Luc still here? And what did it mean that she was glad he was?

The car pulled up outside a small hotel near the harbour. Like most of the places her mother stayed at, it was understated, but exclusive. The modest signage outside was in stark contrast to the luxury to be found once they entered through the glass doors.

She walked through the lobby and immediately spotted her mother sitting at a table near the bar. As always, her mother's coiffured look belied her fifty years, but as Madeleine drew nearer she saw the shock and upset in her eyes. The glass of brandy by her mother's hand told Madeleine something had happened. Her mother drank the occasional glass of wine, but spirits were never her thing.

Sitting in the chair, she appeared to have shrunk in size. Instead of the vivacious woman Madeleine expected, a little mouse had crept into her place. Pale, worried, and scared. It tore at Madeleine's heart. Her previous annoyance over the cancelled Caribbean holiday and her mother not bothering to wait for her to arrive were forgotten in an instant.

Her face brightened when she turned and caught sight of Madeleine. Some of the fear disappeared as she jumped up and hugged Madeleine to her, kissing her on both cheeks.

"Oh Maddie, I'm so glad you made it here so fast. You won't believe what happened. It was awful." Her voice was fraught with emotion as she tried to hold back the tears that flooded her eyes.

"Sit down, Mum, and relax. I'm here now." Madeleine took the seat next to her, presumably recently vacated by her mother's friend. She considered taking a sip of his drink, too, when a glass of red wine appeared in front of her.

Thinking for a moment that her mother had outdone herself with her choice of hotel this time if they could predict their guests' needs, her gaze roamed across the room. Jean-Luc chatted with someone at the bar. He raised his glass at her, and she realised someone was looking after her, but on a far more personal level.

Madeleine relaxed a little as she took a sip. She reached out and took her mum's hand. "What happened?"

"You think you know someone, but then when I spoke to him, I saw a side I'd never seen before." Her mother's voice cracked halfway through the sentence, and Madeleine couldn't make out all of the words.

"Mum, you're not making any sense. Are you saying you saw Charles here?"

Her story came out in a jumble of emotion, sorrow, and anger. She and Gene had decided to go for a stroll whilst they waited for Madeleine. Her mother intimating, of course, that if she'd been here sooner, the whole episode wouldn't have happened.

Somewhere near the marina, they'd literally bumped into Charles. She gestured over towards the bar, and Madeleine realised the man in the sports jacket Jean-Luc was talking to must be Gene.

"He insinuated the most dreadful things would happen to me if I pursued him, Maddie."

"Mum, nothing is going to happen to you." Madeleine

deliberately kept her voice low and spoke slowly, trying to calm her. Her mother wasn't listening. Still too agitated to do anything more than continue to recount her story, she grabbed Madeleine's hand.

"It was such a shock to see him." Her mother's tight squeeze on her hand hurt. "I was just so angry that I forgot everything I'd planned to say, but when he said all those terrible things about me and our life together, I fell apart. When I broached him about the money, he went cold. I mean, really cold Maddie. It was like looking into the eyes of a dead person."

She took a small sip of her brandy, as if to fortify herself to continue. Her voice lowered a fraction. "He told me to watch my step, that accidents happen to old ladies like me." She squeaked on the old bit, and Madeleine couldn't help but think despite the shock of the situation, the feisty side to her mother was starting to shine back through.

"He said who would notice if anything happened to me with only a daughter a thousand miles away who didn't care, but you do care, don't you, Maddie?"

Her mother might be adept when it came to manipulating people's emotions, but Madeleine wanted to wring Charles Jackson's neck for the state he'd put her mother in.

"Mum, of course I do. Who's the one that always comes whenever you call?"

"I was so scared. I didn't know what else to do, so Gene and I came straight back here to wait for you and your friend."

A warm tingling on the back of her neck alerted Madeleine to Jean-Luc's presence before her mother turned to inspect the man who sat down at their table with Gene. Her eyes shifted back to Madeleine's, the dramas of the day forgotten. Reacting to the *how did you manage that?* look her mother gave, Madeleine fought back a wave of annoyance at the unspoken question.

"I think that was the wisest course of action, Barbara." Smoothly interjecting himself into the conversation, Jean-Luc held out his hand. "We spoke on the phone earlier. Jean-Luc Delacroix."

Madeleine swore her mother swooned as she replied, "Enchantée." Great. Her mother had taken one glance at Jean-Luc and cast him in the role of white knight.

"First thing tomorrow, Madeleine and I will take you to the police. We can explain to them what happened and file a report. I think this is a matter for the authorities to investigate." Jean-Luc continued his charm offensive, but it was wasted on her mother, who looked crestfallen.

"The police will take far too long to retrieve my money, and the longer we leave it, the less likely it will be that I'll see any of it again." Barbara stared hopelessly into her glass of wine and sighed. "I'm sorry. You shouldn't concern yourself with my little problems. Maddie and I can manage, can't we, dear?" She reached out and squeezed Madeleine's hand tightly.

Madeleine recognised a mile off what was happening. How come she could see when her mother manipulated someone else, but never realised it until it was too late when she was on the receiving end?

Her mother dabbed her eyes with a tissue and put on her brave face, as Madeleine liked to think of it. "I'm sure I'll get some money back from him eventually, and in the meantime I could always mortgage the house for a little cash to keep me going."

Madeleine didn't like to point out the house was rented.

She was enjoying herself for once, watching two expert manipulators try to outdo each other. Clearly her mother wanted Jean-Luc to go and confront Charles. While Madeleine had no doubt Jean-Luc would be an intimidating presence, she didn't think in these circumstances it would make any difference to the situation.

"Barbara, I insist." Jean-Luc spoke firmly, but patiently. Madeleine admired his persistence, but she still wasn't sure if her mother would get the message. Jean-Luc would never agree to do what she obviously wanted. "There are things you do not yet know about this man. Aspects of his past that may put your life and those around you in danger."

"But I do. I was just telling Maddie he threatened both Gene and I earlier." Her eagerness to bring out Jean-Luc's chivalrous instincts became her downfall, and Jean-Luc wasted no time in pointing out the obvious.

"Then surely you must agree that going to the police is the only option."

"He said things would get nasty if I went to the authorities."

Madeleine sensed this might go on forever if she didn't intervene, and while she found the growing impatience in Jean-Luc's eyes amusing, she took pity on him.

"But if you don't, Mum, how are you ever going to get your money back? It's just threats to bully you. You need to let someone with the authority to take action handle it."

She saw the flicker of thanks in his eyes before he turned his gaze back to her mother to reassure her. "Besides, once you speak to the police, we can take you straight back home. Believe me, he has more pressing issues at the moment than to worry about carrying out any threats."

Over dinner, Madeleine explained to her mother more

about what Jean-Luc had discovered. By the end of the evening, even Barbara agreed that perhaps going to the authorities was the best route. Gene certainly didn't want any further personal involvement with Jackson and thanked Jean-Luc profusely for his assistance as they said their good-byes later on in the lobby.

"Now Mum, don't worry anymore about it tonight, okay?" She hugged her briefly and could tell her mother was back to her old self when she stiffened against having her clothes wrinkled and hair mussed. Madeleine shrugged off the ache in her heart at the rejection. "Jean-Luc and I will meet you here tomorrow morning, but if you need me in the meantime, we're only down the road, so I can always pop back."

JEAN-LUC SHIFTED UNEASILY AS HE WATCHED MADELEINE AND her mother say goodbye. Madeleine's reaction to her mother's brush-off told him so much about why she was determined to avoid relationships. What he didn't know was how he could persuade her that perhaps her point of view was skewed.

CHAPTER 11

3:14 a.m. glowed from his phone. Careful not to disturb Madeleine, Jean-Luc rose from the bed and pulled on the jeans he'd shed a few hours before when he and Madeleine had tumbled into the room.

Had making love seemed a little desolate? More like goodbye, or was he imagining it? He'd sensed Madeleine distancing herself ever since he'd returned home yesterday and found her packed, but he wasn't sure if it was his imagination, a reaction to something he didn't quite understand, or if it was real.

He needed a drink. Heading to the bar on the other side of the hotel suite, Jean-Luc glanced back at Madeleine's sleeping form. Lit up from the shadows of the night by the soft glow from the main room, she looked ethereal, and his heart stood still. His desire grew as he studied her.

The sheet, draped over her body, emphasised her curves. An arm, carelessly thrown out across the bed, exposed a hint of breast, while the other arm on her pillow drew his attention to her long dark tresses. He could still feel the silky touch of her hair as it swung seductively over his chest when she'd ridden them both to an earth-shattering climax earlier.

The memory pulled him back into the room. Screw the drink, he had a better drug in mind. To lose himself in her arms was a sweeter oblivion than alcohol. If she was planning to go back to London, then he wanted to be lodged so deep in her mind that there was no room for anyone else. She might run now, but sooner or later she'd figure it out. He'd always be there for her.

Walking back to the bed, he removed his jeans and studied her for a few moments, before bending down to slide his fingertips over her back as she slept on her side.

Tenderly moving her hair to one side, Jean-Luc kissed the soft skin at the back of her neck, engulfing himself in the scent that drove him mad every time she was nearby. His lips determined their own path as they nibbled their way down the curve of her spine, his tongue dipping into the indent of her lower back, his taste buds exploding with the flavour of her.

The murmured sounds of her appreciation as she awakened fuelled his desire. Her skin was smooth and warm as his fingers roamed, tracing the outline of her breasts, cupping them in his hand, encouraging her nipples into taut peaks. His hands drifted lower, and a smile crossed Madeleine's face as she became fully awake.

"Hmm, would you like a job as my personal masseuse?" Her voice was husky with passion as she reached a hand out and twisted her fingers in his hair.

"You couldn't afford me," he countered. Jean-Luc wanted a permanent position, but he knew Madeleine would only consider a temporary one.

"I could make it up to you in other ways." A sexy smile

crossed her face as she teased him, oblivious to his inner turmoil. She yawned and stretched, before turning around.

When her soft mouth wrapped around his cock as he leaned over the bed, he wasn't sure how much more he could take. His arousal became so intense as she started to suck that it was all he could do to restrain himself from thrusting further in. Looking down into her green eyes as she gazed back at him was the most erotic moment of his life, and he stilled her for fear of losing control.

"As much I love what you're doing to me, chérie, you need to stop." His hands were already in her hair holding the crown of her head to him, but now he gently drew her away and pulled her up onto her knees. He kissed her deeply, wrapping his arms around her tightly, holding her close.

When he sensed her hesitation, he stopped kissing her for a moment and brought their lips just a breath apart. "What's wrong?" The words came out as barely a whisper. He ran his knuckles up and down her back in a comforting gesture. Her eyes were closed, but her forehead was creased in concentration. She was struggling with something—he hoped it was their future.

"Tomorrow," she whispered back, and he shushed her with a finger to her lips.

"Don't, Madeleine." He kissed her eyelids and lowered his lips to her mouth. "Tomorrow will come soon enough, and we can worry about it then. Let tonight be for us." His hands reached up to hold either side of her face. His thumbs rubbed over her cheekbones, memorising every detail, the satin sheen to her skin, the warmth of her blush. Her eyes opened, and Jean-Luc saw the unshed tears there. He took solace that at least she wasn't finding the thought of going away as easy as the impression she'd given earlier.

Her mouth rose in a small, trembling smile, and a glimmer of hope burned within him as he pressed his lips against hers once more. He coaxed her mouth apart with his tongue as his hands continued his earlier exploration of her body, enticing Madeleine to abandon herself to him.

Her soft sighs and caressing touch drove him to new heights, inspired him to want and to give more. As her body reached a fevered pitch, he turned Madeleine around and eased her back onto the bed. His hands smoothed down the arch of her back and held her hips as he teased them both with the tip of his erection. Writhing with passion, she moved backwards to encompass the length of him.

Smiling at her at boldness and revelling in the power of her desire, he took charge once more and with slow deliberate thrusts brought them both to the brink of ecstasy. As Madeleine fell into the dark abyss, Jean-Luc's heart surged as she cried out his name, before his own release consumed him.

THE CAR THEY RODE IN DROVE SMOOTHLY THROUGH THE streets, past the marina, and inland to the airport, where the helicopter waited for them. Inside the limousine it was silent, all of them lost deep in their own thoughts. Gene, Madeleine noticed, hadn't let go of her mother's hand since leaving the police station. *Here we go again,* she thought.

Unbeknownst to her, Jean-Luc had arranged an appointment with the authorities the night before. The seriousness of the situation was apparent as soon as they were shown to a room where several other people already waited for them.

He'd been right. A lot of different organisations wanted to speak to Charles Fairfax Jackson.

From Interpol and two detectives from Paris and London to an official from the Australian embassy and a couple of individuals who deliberately didn't introduce themselves, the room was pretty crowded. A small smile crossed Madeleine's face. She had to hand it to her mother. She knew how to pick them.

The meeting took place in a mixture of French and English. They questioned Barbara and Gene about what had happened in Nice and went over in minute detail their lives in Bergerac, building up a picture of where Jackson lived for the last ten months. After an hour or so, they were thanked, told someone would be in contact, and shown the door.

Madeleine didn't feel as if she understood any more about the situation afterwards than she did going in. It had definitely been a one-way transference of knowledge. She still wasn't sure if her mother's money would be recovered.

Her mother nudged Gene and indicated to something outside the car window. Madeleine took the opportunity to lean across and speak to Jean-Luc softly.

"When did you call the police?"

"As soon as Gene mentioned he and Barbara had seen Jackson. I thought your mother might scare him off, and I wanted to give the authorities a chance to catch up with him."

"Did they?" She moved forward in her seat eagerly awaiting his answer. Perhaps he knew more than he had let on previously.

"I don't think so, but I'm sure it will only be a matter of time." His reassuring tone was meant for her mother, who was now listening to their conversation.

"How come there were so many people there? I thought that it would be a problem to make them take us seriously, or at least until they'd investigated the situation."

"Being the poster boy for entrepreneurism has its advantages." He winked at her, and her stomach somersaulted at the first hint of recognition of the emotion they'd shared the night before. In the rush to get ready this morning, she couldn't decide whether they had genuinely overslept or if it had been a deliberate avoidance tactic on his part.

He shrugged. "I was a credible source of information as soon as I rang. Then it was probably only a couple of clicks on a computer before they appreciated how much they wanted to talk to Jackson."

"I don't suppose you called the front desk either."

"No. There is that, too." The slight rise of his eyebrows confirmed he probably had the chief of police on speed dial.

They boarded the helicopter without delay. It hardly seemed real that she and Jean-Luc had arrived less than twenty-four hours previously.

Despite the morning's shenanigans, her mother spent virtually the entire flight back to the chateau talking as if she didn't have a care in the world. Madeleine was sure she spied the pilot isolating the headphone chatter. Whether her mother realised that Jean-Luc barely responded to her questions or that he and Madeleine hadn't spoken to each other since boarding the helicopter, she wasn't sure. Gene certainly made up for any lack in their responses.

NOT THAT MADELEINE WASN'T GRATEFUL, BUT CHANTAL TOOK control the moment they landed on the lawn behind the chateau. It must be a family trait. Without giving her a chance to say differently, Chantal whisked her mother and Gene away for coffee on the terrace, while Jean-Luc guided Madeleine to the salon where they'd kissed that first day. It seemed like a lifetime ago.

He closed the door quietly and turned to face her. They stared at one another for several moments, not knowing what to say. A deep chasm was about to be ripped through the middle of their fragile relationship, and Madeleine wanted to do anything but confront the truth.

"What happens now?" Jean-Luc's voice gave her the courage to cling to her beliefs. It was firm and steady, devoid of emotion, no hint of the shared memories from the last few days.

Her mother proved to her time and again that romance was a charade, a pleasurable emotion that deluded one or both parties. An illusion that only lasted until the veil of deceit was drawn back, leaving the other person feeling cold, alone, and a little bit afraid. She'd vowed she was never going to be that little girl at boarding school again, waiting foolishly for a small glimpse of love. She couldn't take the risk, not even for Jean-Luc.

Standing up a little straighter, she took a deep breath. "You know what happens next. I take Mum home and leave tomorrow to go back to London."

"And what about us?" Jean-Luc moved over to the window and stared out at the garden beyond. Madeleine saw that like her, he also held himself rigid, as if preparing for a physical onslaught. She stared at his profile, memorising the straight lines of his nose, the curve of his cheekbones, the jut of his chin.

She sighed. "There is no us. We had fun, but it's time to get back to reality. I've a job, a flat, and a life in London."

"Is that all this is, fun?" He turned, but she couldn't meet his gaze. Her heart thumped so rapidly she was sure it would give away the effect the whole conversation was having on her if he peered a little deeper. If he glimpsed even a chink in her armour, he would be able to talk her into something that ultimately wouldn't be good for her in the long term.

"What would you say it was, Jean-Luc?"

He ran a hand through his hair. "I don't know. I thought perhaps you might like to hang around to find out?" The accusation that she was being a coward hung in the air.

"Even if we hadn't gone to Nice, if I had just broken down on the road and not been travelling to see my mother. I would still be going home at the end of my vacation."

"Ok. I admit I haven't really thought the geographies through, but I've never met anyone like you before." He started to pace the room and then paused. "Mon Dieu, I've never even felt this way before. I just want a chance, Madeleine, a chance to show you how good it could be."

She stared down at her hands, wondering what to say next. She didn't doubt being with him would be good, at least for a while, but nothing lasted forever, and for once in her life she didn't think she would survive the disappointment. When he became bored with her, she would be nothing more than another responsibility on his list, and she couldn't do that to herself or him.

His angry gaze bored into her, but his gentle tone surprised her. "Maybe it's here, maybe we meet in London, but you can't keep on running from your emotions forever, Madeleine. Sooner or later, you're going to look in the mirror and see the life you lead isn't as full as you'd like to believe. Without taking chances, you'll never be happy."

It was all the provocation Madeleine needed to stick to her resolve. How dare he think her life was empty just because he wasn't in it! She rounded on him and marched over to where he stood.

"You accuse me of running away from myself, but believe me, I'm well aware of exactly who I am." She pointed towards herself angrily. "I see this face in the mirror every morning. It's the one I saw reflecting back at me every day at boarding school, alone on visiting days. The one that taunted me for being the reason my mother's relationships ended and scathed me for never being enough of a daughter to make her keep me around when someone new came along."

She took a deep breath, calmed herself, and took the sound level down a notch. "But do you know what? That's okay. I'm a big girl. I can live with it, but doing so comes with a certain realism. Rely on no one else for your happiness, for it only leads to disappointment."

"It shouldn't be like that." Frustration tainted his voice.

"No, you're right, but it's a fact. Even when someone cares about you, they still can't be relied upon. Try asking Chantal." She regretted the words as soon as she spoke them, horrified that she had lashed out in such a vicious way. "I'm sorry. That was unforgivable. I gave no regard for the pain you still suffer at not being there for her."

"But it makes your point beautifully." Irony, laced with a bitterness aimed at himself, clouded his voice.

"You're living a life that revolves around Chantal, not your own, and she's trying to find her own way in the world in the shadow of nightmares and not disappoint you." She wrapped her fingers around his arm and squeezed, trying to take the harshness out of her words. "Neither of you are truly happy. So before you accuse me of not taking chances, take a look in the mirror yourself."

JEAN-LUC WAS STUNNED. HE KNEW HER MOTHER'S DISREGARD for her daughter's emotional wellbeing had caused scars, but merde, he didn't he realise how deep it went. Worse still she had a point about Chantal. He didn't let his sister take chances.

He sat down on the chair behind him and put his elbows on his knees, his head in his hands. He needed time to think, to be able to say the right thing. Without doubt he could go over to her right now and kiss her into submission, but they had bigger issues to resolve. Until this moment he hadn't comprehended how insurmountable they seemed.

Who knew, maybe she was right? Everything did revolve around Chantal, but was it love or guilt that made it so? When had the two become a disease that ate into every fabric of his life?

"Sometimes you have to let something go for it to come back to you." He felt her crouch down beside him. It took all his willpower not to reach out, pull her close to him, and end this madness. "Chantal won't break if you let her spread her wings. She may falter, she may make mistakes, but they'll be hers, not yours to regret. She'll grow up and you can find out who you are when you don't have the overwhelming responsibility of protecting someone from the dead." Madeleine stood and moved over to the door.

Her words made time stand still. What did he have to offer her? A man consumed by guilt, overprotective of his sister, unwilling to give up an inch of control. Her accusations were true, but it didn't detract from the certainty that her feelings for him were just as strong as his for her. If he didn't do something soon, then she'd be through the door and gone forever.

He rose and started to pace around the room again.

"You're right, bien sûr. However, I have a question for you, Madeleine. You say you rely on no one for your happiness, but are you happy?" He turned to look at her. Beneath her tan, her face was pale, dark circles began to show under her eyes. "Were you happy when you arrived here? Because I don't think so. If you're not doing such a great job of it, why won't you give others the opportunity to make you happy?"

"You know why." She reached out for the door handle.

"No, I don't think I do." He paused when her hand faltered and forced himself to speak more softly. "Everyone is scared of being alone, but if you don't take a risk, then that's exactly what you're going to be, just going through the motions, not truly living. No one to share the magic with, life's joys, its sadness. Believe me, I've seen them all, and having someone to experience them with, even if they are not here now, makes the memories all the sweeter."

His eyes never left her face. He saw the confusion there, the hesitation, and the tears that spilled over when she could no longer hold the pain of leaving inside.

Slowly she turned the handle, and the door opened.

"Mon Dieu! For once in your life, Madeleine, trust your emotions." He roared so loudly the windowpanes rattled. Madeleine winced, but she stayed where she was. He knew then that he loved her, but he'd lost the battle for her heart.

Somewhere out on the terrace, Chantal offered a little Gallic shrug to her guests. "Chien qui aboie ne mord pas. His bark is worse than his bite," she translated quietly.

· · ·

WHEN MADELEINE ARRIVED OUTSIDE AFTER CHECKING SHE hadn't left anything in her room, her blue Peugeot was in the courtyard. Jean-Luc must have arranged for it to be brought round. Her mother's and Gene's bags were already inside. Only hers remained to be added.

Chantal came up and wrapped an arm around her waist. Tears threatened to overwhelm Madeleine again.

"Take care, chérie, and don't forget to keep in touch. I'm planning my next big adventure in London now that I have a friend there." She gave her a squeeze and kissed her on both cheeks before allowing Madeleine to finish loading the boot. By then her mother and Gene were in the car.

Just as she was ready to leave, Jean-Luc appeared. He leaned in through the open door, standing so close that the scent of him almost made her cave, wanting to believe in something more.

"Remember, ma naïade, I am only a mortal man. It is you that has the power to break the curse." He shut the door, and Madeleine started the journey down the driveway.

Unable to tear her eyes away, she watched him in the rear-view mirror as she rolled down the drive. The memory of him standing there, the imposing, grey stoned chateau rising up behind, and the dark clouds of an oncoming storm replacing the blue sky above, would haunt Madeleine for the rest of her life.

CHAPTER 12

Placing the key in the lock, Madeleine paused and savoured the anticipation as it washed over her. Home at last.

She'd thought about this moment ever since arriving at her mother's house yesterday. Within minutes of stepping out of Madeleine's car, her mother had picked up the phone to answer an invitation to a cocktail party that evening, insisting she needed to get on with her life and put the misery of Charles behind her. Madeleine had done this enough times to know when she, and her rescuing services, were being dismissed.

She'd left early this morning to give herself plenty of time to make her way back to Calais and cross the Channel tunnel. As she sat in her car under sixty meters of water, she tried to forget the events of the last week and caught up on thirty minutes sleep as the train took her back to England.

Her apartment had always been her haven. It offered a stability she'd never felt growing up. A home that provided a constant source of security, something she could rely on. It didn't matter that it wasn't in the best part of town, that some of the furnishings were a little shabby, or that her neighbours were sometimes noisy. At the end of each day, when she shut the door on the rest of the world, no one could destroy the peace she found there.

She turned the key, and the door swung open. The flat lay out before her, just as she'd left it a week ago. The living room and kitchenette beyond, the evening sun streaming in through the windows. Her bedroom in the shadows to the right of her, and the bathroom off to the left. But the buzz she normally got from being home escaped her.

As she closed the door behind her, it seemed like the final conclusion of her French adventure. An amazing few days with an unbelievably sexy Frenchman who consumed her thoughts anytime she let him drift in. A loneliness gripped her, sweeping over her like a dark, taunting shadow.

Memories flooded her, and she wiped away the tears threatening to fall. Every time she shut her eyes, she smelled the mixture of sandalwood and forest that reminded her constantly of Jean-Luc.

She tamped down her emotions with a mental shake of her head and placed her bags in the bedroom before heading for the shower. With the grime of the day's travelling washed away, she fell exhausted into bed and into a deep, dreamless sleep.

Rain beating against the windowpane woke her. She looked at her phone for the time and groaned. How was it possible to sleep for so long and still feel so dreadful? If she'd walked through a sandstorm, her eyes couldn't be more sore, and her throat raged with pain. Perhaps she'd caught a cold in France. She ignored the voice inside her head, mocking her.

Madeleine crawled out of bed and went to the bathroom in search of some aspirin. Hunting through her wash bag, she came across the shower gel she used at the chateau. She cracked the top open slightly and breathed in. The exotic orchid scent filled her nostrils and brought forth a barrage of images. The chateau, the sleepy villages they drove through, dining out under a canopy of stars, flying down to Nice. Each memory featured a Frenchman her subconscious refused to ban. Jean-Luc telling her his darkest secrets down by the river. Meeting him for the first time. Making love.

She gave up pretending everything was okay and slid down the side of the bath, curled herself into a ball, and cried. Her head against her knees, arms wrapped around her legs, her chest heaved with each sob. Tears flowed down her cheeks. The emotions of the last few days poured out of her unchecked until there was nothing left. Wiping her eyes, Madeleine laughed shakily at her own foolishness and stood up. The reflection in the mirror didn't lie. She looked awful, but somewhere deep inside the outburst had brought her peace and resignation. She'd left at the right time. If she was like this now, what would she have been like six months down the line when his interest in her waned?

When her mobile rang in the evening, Madeleine dashed across to the coffee table and grabbed it. Disappointment weighed heavily within when she glanced at the name. Kathy.

No text, no message after nearly seventy-two hours. What did she expect?

"Hi." She forced enthusiasm into her voice.

"Okay, what gives?" Kathy's no-nonsense tone came through loud and clear, belying the thousands of miles they were apart.

"What do you mean?"

"That over-bright greeting and the fact I haven't heard from you except for some weird text message about a Frenchman."

An image of Jean-Luc standing in front of the chateau as she drove away flashed into Madeleine's mind. The impassive expression on his face made her heart clench at the memory. She longed to place her lips on his and be in arms again. A sigh escaped her.

"Uh-oh."

Startled out of her daydream, Madeleine almost dropped the phone.

"What?" She needed to control herself. Kathy was worse than a blood-hound when she thought something was up.

"You've never made that sound before. Hold on." A thud came down the phone line as Kathy dropped her handset.

Madeleine groaned inwardly. It would take her oldest friend moments to break down her resolve not to think about Jean-Luc. The sound of soft footsteps approaching told Madeleine she was returning to the handset.

"Kathy?"

Glass clinked. "I needed more wine."

Madeleine could hear Kathy taking a sip from what she guessed was a glass of red and smiled. At least some things remained the same.

"Okay. I'm comfy now. Start at the beginning."

So she did. She told her how delicious Jean-Luc looked when they first met in the rain. The water glistening in his hair, his eyes so dark you could happily lose yourself in them and never find your way out. The way he teased her about being a water sprite. Their argument over her car. She told her about the chateau, Chantal, going down to the

South of France to pick up her mother. By the time she was finished, Madeleine's eyes were awash with fresh tears.

She didn't tell Kathy about that final hour at the chateau. It hurt too much. Madeleine smiled ruefully to herself when her friend saw right through her.

"So, why did you come back? You're still on leave till at least the end of this week."

"Because it wouldn't have lasted, Kathy." She couldn't stop her voice from cracking. The lump lodged in her throat at holding back her distress was almost painful. "I've seen it so many times with Mum. What's the point of going through all the heartache when it's doomed from the beginning?"

"I know she is your mother, but for heaven's sake, forget about her. She's one in a million."

A long silence down the line followed, and Madeleine braced herself. Her friend didn't pull any punches, but she often paused to weigh up how much people needed to be told before charging in with her opinions.

"Maddie, you might have thought your life was shit at school." Her voice was quietly reassuring, but firm at the same time. Absently, Madeleine wondered if that was what made her so revered by her colleagues. "But we could never believe that you'd come back from the most exotic countries in the world."

"Mum never really wanted me with her. I was just the convenient excuse to make the guy run in the other direction, and hopefully leave her with some money as a guilt-fuelled parting gift."

"Yeah, and my parents only turned up to sports day because it was the thing to be seen doing. I see them less now than I did at boarding school. That's life, Mads. Get over it."

There was the lack of tact which ruined a perfectly good persuasive argument up until that point.

"I'm not being paranoid, I'm being realistic. Look at his life, destroyed by out-of-control emotions."

"Not by his actions, though." Kathy's tone challenged Madeleine's judgement. "From what you've said, he has done more for his family in the last few years than most people do in a lifetime."

"But love still destroyed their happiness in the first place." Madeleine plucked at an invisible strand on the sofa.

"Maybe you've just not seen real love."

"Maybe it doesn't exist." Her fingers moved to smooth the twill, pressing it firmly in a final act of defiance. Her eyes smarted.

Kathy dismissed her concerns with a snort. "If you don't believe in everlasting love, what about us? I've even forgiven you for standing me up for a Frenchman."

Madeleine smiled. Unable to hold back the moisture flowing down her cheeks, she laughed at her friend's teasing. "It was my mother I stood you up for. Besides, we're different."

"Perhaps he is, too." Kathy's voice was serious now. Madeleine could hear her friend's concern for her over the airwaves. "You're making yourself ill by not being with him. How can that be better than taking a chance?"

A stillness came over her. Different memories crowded her thoughts. The lengths he'd gone to when searching for information about Charles Jackson, putting up with her mother's machinations, arranging everything with the police. He'd done all those things for her. No agenda. No ulterior motivation. He'd done it because he wanted to make her life better. She accused him of being controlling, but she'd been so busy nailing down every aspect of her life to make sure she never got hurt again that she never gave love a chance. Kathy was right. The only person standing in the way of her happiness was her.

"I've fucked up, haven't I?"

"Yep. But it's never too late to say you're sorry."

SIX HUNDRED MILES AWAY, JEAN-LUC PUT THE HANDSET DOWN thoughtfully and stared out through the window at the chateau grounds beyond.

He'd resisted calling Madeleine, even texting her. If he intervened and tried to force the issue, she would see the action as part of his controlling streak. All he wanted to do was listen to her voice again, touch the silken skin of her cheek, and feel her soft lips under his. He could still smell her scent on his pillow when he lay awake at night.

Of course, that didn't mean he didn't know she'd arrived back safely in London. He grimaced at the irony. He still wasn't above controlling his sister, though he was trying to relinquish it a little. Madeleine made her view clear. While Chantal was his top priority, there was no room in his life for someone else. He didn't want to believe she was right, but his heart said differently.

Winning Madeleine over wouldn't happen if she believed somewhere along the road she'd be standing there alone. He could curse her mother for making damn sure Madeleine saw love and abandonment as close bedfellows.

Chantal finally starting to grow up was the only good thing to come out of this mess. It was she who suggested Henrique might be looking for an apprentice. He leaned back in the chair and put his feet up on the desk. After the phone call with Henrique, he was convinced Chantal had already run her ideas past the old family friend before getting Jean-Luc to call as if it was his own plan. A ghost of a smile crossed his lips. Perhaps he'd taught her more about manipulation than he realised.

To give Chantal credit, the idea had merit. Henrique assured him it would be a pleasure and an honour to his mother's memory to take Chantal under his wing. With her help he could expand his antiques business by adding an interior design element. Just looking at her work at the chateau was enough of a portfolio for him to recognise that the girl's style made her a natural, and knowing Jean-Luc she'd have good business sense, too. Jean-Luc didn't bother to dissuade Henrique of that theory, so he let the assumption slide. Besides, he knew Henrique's clientele, and they could afford a little expense.

A noise in the hallway alerted him to someone's presence. He turned away from the window.

"Are you still listening at doorways? I thought you grew out of that habit when you turned sixteen."

Chantal breezed in, a smirk confirming that his hunch had been correct. "And?"

"And what?"

"Ooh." She scowled at him. It made a change from the concerned glances she and Danielle had exchanged since Madeleine left. They thought he didn't notice their silent signals or Danielle's eye roll every time he refused to let her clean his room.

Chantal took a step forward and crossed her arms. "You know exactly what. What did Henrique say?"

He sat back in his chair and put his feet up on the desk, raising his eyes upward as if he was trying to find the right words to tell her. He missed their lighthearted exchanges. Ever since the day she'd called to tell him to come home immediately, Chantal had avoided her usual confrontational stance.

He swung his gaze back down at her. "That your tastes were a bit too wild for his clients."

"He did not!" Outrage spread across her face, and Jean-Luc smiled.

He didn't understand why, but the heavy weight of sadness surrounding him was lifting. A small ray of hope flickered from deep within, something which had deserted him recently, particularly in the stillness of the night. Even when he snatched a few hours of sleep, Madeleine filled his dreams. Cruel visions where she'd never left, but then he woke to relive the desolation all over again.

"No, he said he would be delighted to help develop your obvious talents. You start next week and will stay with him and Julie until you settle in."

Chantal rewarded him with a rush of gratitude and launched herself into his arms, knocking his feet off the desk. It was strange how allowing her to take this opportunity felt so good.

"Thank you, thank you, thank you!" She punctuated every word with a kiss on his cheek. "You won't regret it, Jean-Luc, I promise."

"Okay, okay, enough now." Unused to Chantal's display of affection, he released himself from her hug. "And lay off the croissants, you're getting heavy." A sharp slap across the top of his head put them back to their usual brother—sister footing.

Chantal sat in the chair opposite and grew serious. "What about you, Jean-Luc?"

He sighed and ran a hand through his hair. He knew what she was asking, but it seemed the wrong set of dynamics for Chantal to be the one concerned for him. Discussing her problems came naturally, and besides, he didn't want to share his.

"Sometimes you need to let something go for it to come back to you." His throat tightened with every word. No way was he going to break down in front of Chantal. He coughed. "Madeleine told me that the day she left. At the time, I thought she meant you. Now I'm not so sure."

"You need to speak to her."

You don't know how much. He sat upright and repeated what he told himself every time he reached for the phone. "I'll give her a week."

"Why? What's going to happen then?"

Chantal leaned forward in her chair, her eyes never once leaving his. He saw the sympathy in them, but they also said she thought he was wrong.

He shrugged. "I figure it's a bit like the car. If I force the issue she'll only dig her heels in further. This way, she has time."

"You mean the two of you are as stubborn as each other."

"I'm not stubborn."

Chantal raised an eyebrow. "No? Perhaps it's because no one ever defies what you say, Jean-Luc. What does she need time for?"

"What do you mean?"

"You said this way she has time."

"Time to see thing more clearly."

"You mean your way." Her gaze didn't falter.

A tinge of aggravation invaded his bloodstream. No one ever questioned his decisions, and certainly not Chantal. He cocked his head to dismiss her. "Haven't you got some packing to do?"

"Just telling you how it is, my brother." She kissed his cheek and left the room.

THE PHONE'S BEEP ANNOUNCED A NEW TEXT MESSAGE, AND Madeleine forced herself not to rush over to the coffee table to check. It was all she'd done for the last couple of days since her chat with Kathy, and it only irritated her more.

She sat back on the sofa and carried on watching breakfast TV, but her mind wouldn't switch off. She fidgeted, struggling to get comfortable. She plumped the cushion with so much force it sent a cloud of dust upwards. The least he could do was find out how she was. Thump. *But you told him it was the end. How will he know you've changed your mind unless you tell him?* Double thump.

With a sigh, she gave into temptation and snatched up the phone. At the words on her screen, her heart sank.

Chance to get my money back. Text me when you get to Nice.

Just what was it with her mother? She didn't even try to disguise this latest request with her poor woe-is-me-act. In fact, it wasn't even a request. Her mother might know she still had holiday left and was just sitting at home, but she could've at least jazzed up the message with a please.

As she clicked on the availability link, Madeleine realised she truly was worse than Pavlov's dog. Her mother had conditioned her to respond regardless of the legitimacy or fairness of the request. Within two minutes of receiving the text, she was checking the internet to book a flight. She could resist going, if only to make a point, but then she risked her mother doing something stupid and causing her more hassle.

The plane left around lunchtime. If she hurried, she'd make it to the airport on time. No way would she make the mistake of driving down this time. She texted back her arrival time and walked into the bedroom to pack an overnight bag.

The thought of returning to France caused her heart rate to speed up, or, rather, returning to one Frenchman in particular. She'd picked up the phone several times in the last couple of days to talk to him, but each time she'd bottled out. Now at least she had an excuse to call.

Perhaps it was time to admit to herself she was scared. Apprehensive of going forward, but more afraid of staying where she was. Her perfect life, her own small flat, a good job, and great friends lay shattered like an illusion the moment they didn't include Jean-Luc.

Did he love her? Her mind filled with doubt. But who was to say he wasn't afraid, too?

There was only one way to find out. *Stop being chicken and take a chance.*

A text confirmed her flight was on time. Glancing at the clock, Madeleine realised she was wasting minutes. She locked up the flat and rushed to catch a cab. Hopefully, there would be just enough time to call Jean-Luc before she got on the plane.

JEAN-LUC GRABBED HIS PHONE OFF THE DESK. ONE MISSED CALL. Madeleine. He cursed himself for forgetting to pick up his mobile when he was called into a last-minute meeting.

A rush of dread and adrenaline clashed in his body,

making his stomach churn. Had she changed her mind or was it because the police had been in touch with her? Maybe Chantal was right, and he should have gone after Madeleine sooner or at the very least contacted her. Not ignore her as if she didn't exist in his thoughts every minute of every day. He'd barely slept, barked at anyone who disturbed him. Even his PA ducked her head down every time he walked past. Chantal told him that waiting for Madeleine to contact was irrational, but he wanted Madeleine to come to him, to trust her feelings.

But now staring down at the voicemail icon that winked back at him, taunting him, he wished he'd chased after her, because he wasn't sure he had the courage to listen to the message. At least if he'd followed her to London, he would still hold some control over the situation. He sighed. That was precisely why he hadn't.

He tapped the icon and paced across the room, holding the phone to his ear. The answering service took forever to kick in. He was ready to start shouting at the phone when suddenly Madeleine's voice filled his head and he stood still. She sounded nervous in her greeting. It reminded him of the first time they'd met on the road. Perhaps she wasn't sure of the reception her call would receive.

You should have gone after her.

He sat back down behind his desk. His pulse raced with the anticipation of what she might say. Resting his elbows on the solid wood surface, he slumped his head in the palm of his empty hand.

"I might have made a mistake." She said it so quietly he almost missed it.

His breath caught in his chest. Finally.

He waited for her to continue, but Madeleine stopped

talking. There was a long pause. All he heard was her light breathing and what sounded like a flight announcement in the background.

Then she spoke again. "I have to go. I can't explain now…I'll try to call again later."

Frustration ran through him at missing the call. He tapped the phone to listen to the message again. It was so good to hear her voice. The hope he'd shuttered away poured forth, and he leaned back in his chair. He needed a moment to get a hold of his feelings. The relief that rolled through him left him feeling drained.

She might have made a mistake. A smile spread across his face. The sound of her voice, even though it had only been a few days since he'd heard it, washed over him, filling him with pleasure.

Hairs on the back of his neck tingled as realisation hit. The announcement was in French, not English, and it was flight arrivals. She was in France. What the hell?

He hit dial. Straight to voicemail. "Putain!"

His phone beeped. While listening to Madeleine, he'd missed another call. His blood ran cold as he listened to the message.

CHAPTER 13

Standing in the middle of the arrivals hall at Nice airport, Madeleine stared down at the phone in her hand, willing it to ring. She'd gotten herself so worked up during the flight about calling Jean-Luc that when the call went to voicemail she'd made a mess of the message.

Who tries to say they love someone with the words, I think I made a mistake? It was hardly the most romantic start to a conversation. It didn't say, I've been thinking about nothing but us since the moment I left you. Or can we go back to the beginning and try again? This time I promise to trust that my emotions are real and that yours are, too. No, instead she sounded like someone who'd made an unfortunate shopping purchase.

She smiled at the thought of walking into a boutique and trying to order a Jean-Luc.

A surge of people bustled back and forth, jostling her from one foot to the other. She struggled to keep her balance while she debated what to do next. Would she look needy or just idiotic if she called again? Neither was appealing.

Perhaps she'd find out what her mother was up to and then call him back.

"I'll take that."

Madeleine whirled around, startled by the person who reached across in front of her and snatched her mobile out of her hand.

"Charles?" He appeared different from the photos her mother had showed her, but she was certain it was him. Surprise and confusion clouded her thoughts.

An unease came over her when his hand gripped her upper arm and propelled her forward towards the exit.

"What are you doing? Where's my mother?" She tried to stop walking and shake him off, but the force of his shoulder and chest behind her prevented Madeleine from putting up much of a fight.

"Just be a good girl and come with me quietly."

The sensation of his breath on the back of her neck when he spoke caused the hair there to rise in silent alarm. Adrenalin pumped through her veins in response to the chill that went down her spine. She glanced around the arrivals hall, wondering if she should shout out.

"Don't make a scene. It wouldn't be wise."

His threatening tone silenced her until he forced her into a waiting taxi. Not that anyone appeared to be taking any notice of them, despite his steely hold on her arm. She wasn't sure help would be forthcoming, even if she did say anything. Everyone was too engrossed in their own lives. Just as she had been.

When she heard him tell the driver to take them to the marina, Madeleine relaxed a little. At least it was still a public place.

"Where's my mother? What have you done with her?" She tried to keep the alarm out of her voice.

"All in good time. Just be patient." He shot her a warning scowl to keep quiet, indicating the driver.

"You'd better not have harmed her." She kept her tone low, so her words could only be heard between the two of them.

His lips raised upwards, the expression too patronising to be considered a smile. "I assure you, as far as I know, your mother is quite well."

The car sped its way through the streets and reached the marina before Madeleine could question him further.

"We're here." He leaned over and opened the car door, prodding her to move.

The smell of sea air, mixed with the expensive scent of over-polished motor cruisers, brushed past her on the breeze as she got out of the taxi.

"Where are we going now?" The marina wasn't as busy as she'd hoped it would be, and fear seeped back into her bones.

"To find your mother, of course." He paid the taxi and indicated a large cruiser a short way down.

Madeleine wavered. Her mother's text had said she'd found a way to get her money. She was sure the trip would involve a meeting with Jackson at some point, but she didn't expect to be greeted by him.

Something didn't seem right. Should she follow him and go to her mother, or turn around now and hope she could summon help to find her later?

"Don't waste my time, Madeleine."

The veiled threat made her mind up for her, and she turned to face the boat. No way was she leaving her mother alone with him. If they stuck together, she was sure they'd be able to get away from Jackson.

She climbed aboard the sleek cruiser, following Jackson across the deck and down the steps into the lower cabin.

The room was empty.

"For the last time, where's my mother?" She forced out a much braver, more authoritative tone than she felt.

"I've no idea. Probably playing bridge with her cronies in Bergerac."

"In that case, I'm leaving." She walked back to the steps, but Jackson stepped in her way, blocking her exit with his large frame. He reached into his jacket and drew out a gun. Fear ripped through her, and she froze in the middle of the cabin. Her heart pounded in her throat.

"Sit down over there and be quiet."

Shock and confusion made it hard to catch her breath. "But she texted me to say meet her in Nice."

"No, I did that." His lips rose marginally and his eyes narrowed as if he was talking to someone slightly dim. "Spoofing a text to make a message seem like it's come from someone else is very easy, you know. People are so distrustful of email these days, but not mobiles. If the caller ID appears okay, everyone assumes that's who the sender is."

He leaned back against the galley, placing the weapon beside him on the counter. "I knew you'd be the dutiful daughter and come straight away. As an added incentive, I timed the message so you'd just make the City Airport flight if you hurried. It's amazing how putting a time pressure on stops people from thinking clearly and encourages them to follow orders."

"But I texted my mother back."

He shrugged, unconcerned. "Today is bridge day. I don't suppose she's even turned on her phone in the last several hours."

Her heart sank. He was right. Her mother never checked her mobile at the best of times.

"Anyway, it doesn't matter. I'm sure we won't have long to wait for lover boy to come to your rescue."

Madeleine frowned. "What on earth are you talking about? No one knows I'm here."

"Well, that was foolish of you." He raised his eyebrows and picked up the gun again.

She gulped. Shit.

"Fortunately for you, I made a call. I'm sure Delacroix will arrive in the next half hour or so."

"Jean-Luc? What's he got to do with this?" It was getting more confusing by the moment. She still couldn't get her head around the fact it wasn't her mother who'd texted her.

"He's bringing me a little holiday money since I'm short on cash. I must say, you did well for yourself. I bet it surprised your mother. She always described you as pliable, without much gumption."

The jibe struck home and hurt, but it gave her the impetus she needed to get herself fired up and out of here, before Jean-Luc walked into this nightmare. She stared stony-faced at him, determined not to give away how she felt about her mother's betrayal.

"How did you find out about us? We've only just met."

"The two of you were snapped by paparazzi boarding the helicopter with your mother. It gave me the idea."

His mobile beeped. When he peered down to read the text, Madeleine took her chance to run, but his reactions were too fast. An arm snaked round her neck, pulling her back into the cabin before she even got her foot on the first step.

She bit down hard, her teeth sinking into his skin. He cursed loudly and spun her around. The blow from the muzzle of the gun knocked her sideways. The force sent shooting pains through her cheekbone and into her eye socket. It dazed her for a moment.

He pushed her over the table and pulled her hands behind her. The rope was rough against her wrists as he tied them tightly. Then he hauled her up by the back of her T-shirt and sat her down on the bench seat opposite the galley.

"Next time I won't be so easy on you." His menacing tone left her with no uncertainty that he meant it.

He went back to his mobile phone, tapping away furiously before stowing the device in his pocket and reaching for the gun again.

They stared at each other in silence. Her head pounded. Did Jean-Luc realise it was a trap? She wasn't thinking straight. He must know if he was bringing cash. She needed to get her head together if she was going to get out of this mess alive. Ironic that it was all her own making this time and not her mother's.

If she hadn't been so scared of Jean-Luc rejecting her, she'd have phoned him days ago and avoided this fiasco. *If you'd had the guts to stay in the first place, Jackson wouldn't have stood a chance.* Hold on.

"How did you know I'd be at home?" She dreaded the answer. Madeleine didn't put it past her mother to have been in touch with Jackson anyway.

He shrugged as if it was too simple a question for him to reply. "I rang the chateau saying I had a parcel to be delivered to you. The person answering the phone informed me

you'd already left for London. I called your mother at Bergerac just in case and got the same response."

Madeleine breathed a sigh of relief. At least her mother
hadn't deliberately given away her whereabouts to this
creep.

She looked out of the window. From this vantage point,
she could make out the boat next to them, but nothing more.
The darkened glass prevented anyone from seeing inside, so
even if she did spot someone, it was unlikely she'd be able to
get their attention subtly. The thought depressed her.

A noise from the top deck made her turn her head
towards the steps.

"At last." Jackson pointed the gun at Madeleine. "I was
starting to wonder what was taking you so long, Delacroix."

Jean-Luc. Her heart leapt at the sight of him and then
lurched as she realised the danger he was in.

THE STENCH OF DESIGNER AFTERSHAVE ASSAULTED JEAN-LUC'S
senses as he crept down the steps. He moved slowly to give
his eyes time to adjust to the dimness of the cabin. The situation was as he'd feared.

The blood pumping through his body ever since Jackson's call turned to ice as he caught sight of Madeleine's
white, shocked face.

She sat still as if afraid to move, her hands presumably
tied behind her. Her hair and clothes were in disarray. When
he drew closer, he could see a bruise starting to form on her
cheek. His breath lodged in his throat, and his right fist
clenched. What had the bastard done to her?

"Have you got the money?"

The gravelly voice set Jean-Luc's teeth on edge. He transferred his gaze to Jackson standing by the galley, willing the anger that threatened to overcome him to abate. Now was the time for clear thinking. He could satisfy his urge to beat the living daylights out of the sleazebag later.

Jean-Luc regarded Jackson with cold disdain. He recognised the type, and had been avoiding them on the Riviera for years. They made his skin crawl. Everything they wore, from their clothes to their ostentatious jewellery, was designed to show off their wealth. A paunch from overindulgence and a reddened nose further confirmed it. Their stories were normally as fake as their money.

He lifted the black attaché case he carried. "It's all here, thirty thousand euros." He needed to stall for time. The police were on their way, but Jackson wasn't stupid. He hadn't given away his location until he was sure Jean-Luc had come alone and was only a few steps away on the marina. "Though I'm curious as to why you didn't ask for more."

"It's a case of understanding how much someone like you can lay their hands on without others raising an eyebrow." His conceited tone said it all. He thought he was the master of some complex heist instead of a common conman. Jean-Luc wanted to encourage the attitude, knowing ultimately it would be Jackson's downfall.

Jackson motioned for him to step forward and drop the bag. "Ask for too much and you'd be tempted to go to the police, or someone would be compelled to report it to the authorities."

Without taking his eyes off Jean-Luc, his weapon still pointing at Madeleine, he opened the bag and drew out a handful of notes. His lip rose in a satisfied smile.

Jean-Luc resisted the urge to move too soon and wipe it

off his face. He couldn't afford the risk that Jackson's first reaction wouldn't be to shoot Madeleine.

"But it's nothing compared to what you've taken in France alone?" He tried to insert a tone of admiration into his voice and almost choked on his words.

"My, my, you've been doing your homework." He zipped up the bag and stood back next to Madeleine. "I only need it for cash flow. I was planning on leaving the day I met Barbara and that fool Gene on the marina." A look of annoyance crossed his face. "But your meddling afterwards made it too difficult without showing my hand."

He nodded, indicating Madeleine. "I figured it might be easier if I had a little leverage. And if I was doing that, you might help with some cash to tide me over."

"Spent the rest already?" Jean-Luc couldn't hold back the sarcasm any longer.

Jackson laughed. "You really think I'm that stupid? Why spend it, when it will only give away where it's hidden? Besides, people keep on giving me more." He glanced pointedly at the bag between them. Jean-Luc mentally restrained himself. A violent side he didn't know existed within him itched to be let loose.

"Yes, that's something I've been puzzling. How did you manage to get the money in the first place?" Madeleine's voice came over clear and strong, and Jean-Luc released a sigh inwardly, thankful that, despite appearances to the contrary, she still had the capacity to fight. He knew only too well the tilted angle of her head and the challenging regard in her eyes as she studied Jackson.

"By capitalising on the banks' stupidity." A gloating expression came over Jackson's face. "People think they are making an investment, so it's completely natural to make out a cheque to a bank. But I only need to sign the back of it for the bank to pay the money into my account."

Madeleine gasped. "It's as easy as that?"

"Well, it is until they close the loophole." His voice took on a frustrated resonance.

"Hence the need to change countries." Jean-Luc leaned against the wall of the cabin, trying to appear far more nonchalant than he felt.

Comprehension crossed Jackson's face, and Jean-Luc realised he may have given too much away. He didn't want Jackson to catch on that they knew all about his escapades across the globe, or else he'd be certain that Jean-Luc would've called the police before stepping onto the boat. They needed the element of surprise if they were to get off the boat alive. He had to keep Jackson talking.

"Nice boat. Yours?"

Jackson smirked. "A parting gift from a wealthy widow."

Jean-Luc would lay money she wasn't as rich now as she thought she was.

"We're wasting time." Jackson picked up the attaché case and threw it further down the boat, out of sight.

"So what's your plan?" Where the hell were the police? They should be here by now. He could sense he and Madeleine were fast running out of options.

Last time they were together, he'd tried to convince her she could trust him to always be there for her. He was here now, but it wasn't doing either of them much good. Frustrated at his lack of action, Jean-Luc wanted to punch something, or someone.

"We'll all take a trip out of the marina. Once I'm in open water you two can take the inflatable. By the time you raise the alarm, I'll be long gone."

"Leave Madeleine and just take me."

"I don't think that would be sensible, do you? Of course, if you're growing bored of the girl, you could always leave her with me. I realise now why Barbara didn't want to introduce us before." He reached over to touch Madeleine's cheek with the back of his hand.

She visibly flinched, whether from pain or disgust Jean-Luc didn't know or care. Ever since Jackson had called him earlier that afternoon, he'd been fighting the anger and fear that threatened his equilibrium at the thought of anything happening to Madeleine. At Jackson's insinuation, he couldn't hold back the tide of rage coursing through his veins. When Jackson lowered his gun, momentarily distracted, Jean-Luc charged.

THE TWO OF THEM CAME CRASHING ACROSS THE TABLE IN FRONT of Madeleine, startling her. The breath whooshed out of Jackson as Jean-Luc landed on top of him. Madeleine scrambled out of the way, hindered by her hands that were still tied behind her back. There was no way she'd make it off the boat quickly unless she freed them. She twisted her hands until the rope burned her wrists, but no matter how hard she tried, it didn't loosen.

Jackson recovered rapidly from Jean-Luc's surprise attack and sat up, pushing him backwards with force. He landed against the side of the galley with a grunt. Jackson followed, fists raised. Jean-Luc feinted left and moved right, away from the steps, neatly avoiding the jab. Both men were panting hard, determining their next move.

A clattering on the floor drew their attention. Jackson's gun had fallen from wherever it'd been thrown when Jean-Luc careered into him. It laid only a couple of feet from Jackson, but Madeleine was closer. Her heart slammed against her ribcage. The thought of Jean-Luc being shot sent a surge of adrenalin through her. She kicked it and watched, mesmerised, as the glint of metal slid across the cabin and under the seat. Too bad she didn't think to kick it towards Jean-Luc.

"Fucking bitch!" Jackson turned. His face contorted in anger. He reached out and grabbed a handful of her hair with his left hand. An agonising pain slashed through her, and she screamed as her head jerked back. He raised his right fist, and she braced herself for the impending agony.

The sound of bone meeting cartilage cracked through the air, and with a yell, Jackson let her go. She slumped to the floor. A spasm shot up her spine, making her gasp.

Above her, Jean-Luc and Jackson were circling each other, fists raised. Blood covered Jackson's face, the result of Jean-Luc's punch. A small cheer of victory rose inside her, swiftly tempered by the reality of the situation. If they were to take Jackson down, she needed to get off the boat to raise the alarm.

With a last excruciating pull on the rope, her hands became free. She stumbled upright.

"Allez, Madeleine." Jean-Luc's exclamation distracted Jackson, and he scored another hit. She watched in fascination as Jackson's head went back at an abnormal angle. "Run!"

His shout galvanised her into action. She started up the steps, but Jean-Luc's punch forced Jackson closer to her. His hand grabbed at her ankle, pulling her back down. She twisted and turned, trying to dislodge his grip, willing her numb hands to find something on the upper deck that she could get a purchase on and pull herself away from him.

There was a loud thump, followed by a groan, and her ankle was free. She didn't stop to see what had happened, but kept climbing to the top.

Sunlight blinded her after the low light levels of the cabin. Her lungs felt as if her chest was about to explode. Every breath came in racking gasps as she tried to suck in more oxygen, but there was no time to rest. Driven by fear for Jean-Luc, she rushed across the deck and onto the marina. It took her a moment before she saw the police further round the dock and shouted to draw their attention.

Staggering towards them, the noise of an engine starting her made her turn around. Jackson was undoing the slip ropes and preparing to leave the mooring. Where was Jean-Luc? She scanned the rest of the boat, searching for him.

The cruiser was half-way out of the quay when he appeared on deck looking disoriented. By then, police were swarming on the quayside, guns drawn.

Jean-Luc grabbed Jackson by the scruff of his shirt and hauled him backwards, away from the helm. The two of them fell on the deck. They continued to fight. Frustrated that she couldn't see what was happening this far away, Madeleine ran to the edge of the empty dock.

Before the police dinghy reached the cruiser, Jackson stood. Then Jean-Luc's frame appeared, bent double, his arm clutching his ribs. Madeleine's heart twisted at his obvious pain. He stared down at the palm of his hand like he expected to see blood, and her breath caught in her throat.

A single blow was all it took for Jackson to send Jean-Luc over the side and into the harbour water. Madeleine stood paralysed as the boat turned just a fraction and clipped the side of his head.

"Jean-Luc!" She screamed as he disappeared under the water.

Madeleine gulped back the sobs that threatened to overtake her. She stared transfixed as the police boat reached the spot Jean-Luc had gone under and a diver slid into the water. Tears rolled down her cheeks. Moments later, they pulled Jean-Luc's lifeless body out of the marina. The diver looked across the water at his colleagues and almost imperceptibly shook his head.

A cold clammy sweat shook through her body. Bile rose in her throat. She threw up before falling into a dead faint.

CHAPTER 14

A loud beep drifted into his consciousness, bringing Jean-Luc out of the hazy fog he wallowed in. The unpleasant smell and rough sheets of the hospital bed jarred as much as the pain in his head.

He groaned. The last time he'd felt like this had been twenty years ago when Raph had dared him to climb to the highest point on a sweet chestnut tree. He'd fallen and knocked himself out after his head collided with a branch on the way down.

He didn't want to open his eyes. The light hurt too much. Everything hurt too much. Except for the delicate hand in his. That felt good. His heart clenched at what it might mean.

He tried to speak but couldn't. The hand moved and then touched his brow in a soothing gesture. The aroma surrounding him changed from clinical disinfectant to an intoxicating, exotic flower. He inhaled deeply to assuage his desire over the last week to smell her sweet perfume once more. An excruciating pain radiated across his chest, but he didn't care. He'd rather die in agony than not breathe in the scent of her again.

Warm lips kissed his forehead, and he sighed. The pain subsided.

She cupped his head and pressed a glass to his lips. Cool water trickled over his tongue. This was what it must be like to be found, lost in a desert. His head was gently lowered back against the pillow.

He tried to speak again. The soreness in his throat almost stopped him, but he needed an answer to a question that had plagued him since Jackson's call.

"I got your message." His voice was raspy, unreal, like it wasn't his. "The mistake… was it us or you trying to get yourself killed?"

There was a long pause before the hand touched his brow again, brushing away his hair.

"Shh, Jean-Luc. We'll talk later."

He shook his head slightly with impatience and wished he hadn't. Blinding lights flashed behind his eyes, and the migraine intensified.

"Now." He didn't have the energy for more words. He held his breath, waiting for her answer, hoping it was the one he wanted to hear.

"Us." The voice drifted down to him like a gentle melody. Delicate fingers were touching his again.

He could sleep now.

NEXT TIME HE WOKE, THE FOG SURROUNDING HIM HAD LIFTED. He hurt everywhere, but a vitality hummed through his body with an energy brought about by the certain knowledge Madeleine had returned because of him.

He opened his eyes slowly to the dimly lit room, waiting for the light to make his head explode. When it didn't, he tried to sit up. The pain in his side deepened, and he remembered the knife Jackson had stuck between his ribs. Muttering a curse, he eased back onto the pillow.

A movement across the room made him turn his head. Madeleine was curled up in a visitor's chair, sleeping soundly. She looked exhausted. He longed to reach out and comfort her, to run his fingers through the silky strands she wore like a veil across her face.

After Jackson's message, he was convinced that he'd misinterpreted her voicemail and she'd only returned to France to help her mother.

All he'd thought about on the way down south was what a fool he was for not going after her sooner. If he had, she wouldn't have been in danger. His gut knotted as he remembered the fear that something would happen to her before he turned up.

It was lucky he had still been at the factory when Jackson's call had come through. It was close enough to an airfield to borrow a plane rather than rely on his helicopter, saving him at least an hour. He couldn't allow himself to think about what might have happened if he'd arrived later.

The noise of the heartbeat monitor started to pick up. He needed to calm himself, or the place would be swarming with medical staff, and he liked it just how it was. Alone with Madeleine.

She stretched and opened her eyes, her gaze immediately searching for his. She smiled shyly at him, and his heart leapt.

"I thought I'd lost you." He spoke without thinking. Until now, he'd only thought about the shock, anger, and fear that had coursed through his blood in the last twenty-four hours. Or had it been longer? He wasn't really sure how long he'd been unconscious.

Her face became serious under his intense scrutiny. "You're not the only one. When you went under the water…" She faltered, her eyes were shimmering with tears.

"I meant before."

"I know."

The paleness of her skin and the luminosity that shone from her green eyes made her appear every bit the fragile, petite naïade. He longed to pick her up from the sagging chair she sat in and carry her away to where no one could harm her. Not her mother, nor the bastards she associated with.

"Come here." He held out his hand.

She stood and walked gracefully towards him, sitting on the edge of the bed. He reached up to caress her cheek. Anger ripped through him as he saw the dark bruise on the cheek opposite. The fall of her hair had made it impossible to see from across the room. He gently touched the discoloured skin.

She winced. "He hit me with his gun when I tried to run."

He froze. He hadn't gotten there in time after all.

"Don't do it, Jean-Luc." She squeezed his forearm, her eyes insisting he listen to her.

"What?"

"Torture yourself that you weren't there. I can see it in your eyes. You can't be everywhere at once. Sometimes bad things happen, and there's nothing anyone can do about it."

"But I should have been there."

"You were there for me, Jean-Luc. Don't ever doubt that."

She gave him a faint smile. "Admittedly, you could have arrived ten minutes earlier."

"Merde. I've missed you every day you've been gone, mon ange. For days I've resisted calling you or texting you." He gestured to her cheek, not daring to touch it again. "When I think a few minutes might have saved you this pain, my heart grows heavy."

A tear rolled down her other cheek, and he wiped it away with his thumb. She leaned into his palm, and a sensation of peace came over him.

"What changed your mind?" He needed to hear it from her. To be certain she didn't doubt that his love would be everlasting. He smiled to himself. As if he could stop the tidal wave of emotion that surged within him every time she was in his thoughts, let alone in the same room.

A frown crossed her face, and a flicker of unease settled in his gut. Maybe she was still not certain.

"Do you remember the day we visited the caves?" She sat back, moving away from his hand.

He understood her need for distance. When they were together, he couldn't think straight, and this was undeniably the time for coherent thought.

"I'd never been so aware of someone before, so swept along by emotion. It scared me." She stood and paced across the room. "Not that I would admit it. I told myself it was nothing more than a holiday romance. A little light-hearted fun with a sexy guy. I convinced myself it felt different because I hadn't been with anyone in a while."

"A lack of lovers doesn't create the sexual chemistry we share, Madeleine."

Her blush reminded him of the first night they'd dined

together, when only his conscience stood between him and his desire to take Madeleine on the kitchen table.

"Everything moved so fast. Suddenly it wasn't a fling any more. I was starting to care for you too much, and you must understand that's never worked out well for me." She wrapped her arms around herself as if to ward off an invisible chill that had settled in the room. "I didn't think I'd survive the heartache if I stayed." Madeleine spoke so low he only just heard the words.

"So you ran." His voice strained against the tightness of his throat.

"I've been running since we first stopped outside the chateau."

Hope started to burn within him again. "And now?"

"When I arrived home, I realised it didn't matter. I'd left it too late, and my heart was in ruins anyway. It drove home that the only person preventing me from having what I want is me."

"And what is it you want?"

"You."

He groaned.

"What is it?" She rushed over to him, concern written across her face.

"I want to hold you in my arms. I want to kiss you senseless. I want to make love to you again. I'm so hard for you that I can't believe the one part of me that isn't injured is so painful." He banged his fist against the bedsheets in frustration. "Mon Dieu, I can't even sit up."

The shrill alarm of the heartbeat monitor interrupted him.

"Merde."

Within seconds a nurse came in, reset the alarm, and

started to take his vital signs. He gave the nurse a stare that normally sent people scurrying away, but she ignored him and continued her work. When his impatience started the heart monitor alarm off again, she glared at him pointedly before returning to her charts.

He needed to finish talking to Madeleine. There was still so much to resolve. He'd had enough with fussing.

"Fiche le camp!"

"That's no way to talk to the nurse. She's only doing her job." Chantal breezed in, and for a moment he was confused.

"What?" She raised her hands, palms outward. "You think I wouldn't come running to see my favourite brother just because I've a splendid new job with all of Paris at my feet?"

She kissed both his cheeks and then went and hugged Madeleine. It was absurd to be so envious of his sister's mobility just because he desperately wanted to hold Madeleine himself. Frustrated, Jean-Luc turned his scowl on Chantal.

Her face lit up into a smile as she glanced between him and Madeleine. Taking the nurse by the arm, she led her out of the room.

"We'll come back later."

The door swung shut behind her.

"Chantal told me what you did for her." Madeleine sat back down on the bed and took his hand in hers. It felt warm compared to when he'd first arrived at the hospital. He'd been so cold that she'd refused to believe the hospital staff when they'd said he was still alive.

"I should have done it sooner. You were right when you said I needed to let her make her own mistakes."

Her stomach flipped when she remembered how she lashed out at him. "I was wrong to interfere when I couldn't even face up to my own faults." If she'd been responsible for Jean-Luc's death, she would never be able to look Chantal in the face again. The emotions she'd experienced when she'd seen his lifeless body pulled from the water flooded back and reduced her to tears in an instant.

His thumb rubbed back and forth over her knuckles. "So tell me more about this sexy guy?" A teasing glint reflected in his eyes.

"What?"

He grinned. "You said you wanted a little light-hearted fun with a sexy guy."

Incredible. She was berating herself about how much harm she'd caused him, and he was picking up on entirely the wrong points of their conversation.

"I'm not feeding your ego." She stood and peered through the internal window at the nurses' station a short way down the corridor. Lifting a hand, she wiped away the tears from hers eyes. "It's going to be huge after the nursing staff have finished with you judging by the way they've been in and out since we arrived."

"Jealous, chérie?"

She gave the answer his response deserved and ignored the question.

"Of course, you might just have reduced your odds a bit by shouting at the last one to get out." She couldn't keep the sarcasm from her voice.

"I wanted to be alone with you." Jean-Luc's voice was quiet.

Madeleine swung around. All traces of humour were wiped from his face. He'd been protecting her again, this time from her own morbid thoughts.

The stark contrast of his tanned cheek against the pillow as he turned his head made her realise his earlier pallor had vanished. His eyes blazed with deep emotion, and a small thrill went up her spine. It gave her the courage she needed to continue.

"I thought I'd lost you when you fell into the water." Her throat constricted with the pain of holding back tears. "That I'd never get to tell you how much I loved you."

"You can tell me now." He held out his hand to her.

She walked back to the bed and clasped it firmly. It was the lifeline she needed at this moment in time.

Madeleine took a deep breath. "When I left the chateau, I took something that didn't belong to me."

His forehead creased in confusion.

"I stole your heart and your love, and I didn't deserve either."

"I gave them willingly."

Her lips rose in a slight smile at his sweet words, and her heart rode up to form a lump in her throat. "I didn't earn them."

"Love is not something to be earned, Madeleine." He squeezed her hand, his gaze never faltering from hers.

She could lose herself in those eyes, so dark, so full of promise. "I truly believed leaving you was the right thing to do." Her heart thumped madly. "Until I arrived home." She struggled to breathe at the admission. "Everything I thought I wanted turned out to be just an empty shell. You offered me a chance at happiness, and I turned you down. At the car when we said goodbye, you trusted my love would be enough to bring me back before I even knew myself. But I gave you nothing in return. Not even hope." A wretchedness built inside her at the memory.

"Come here, chérie." He held his arms open for her to rest on his chest, and she couldn't resist. Safe in his embrace, a lone tear fell.

"I was in love with you but too scared to admit it to myself and even more afraid to say it you."

His fingers massaged her scalp, soothing her. "Scared of what, mon coeur? You are afraid of nothing, n'est-ce pas?"

"Rejection. That I'd tell you and then after a while you'd get bored and move on."

His hands gripped her shoulders and pushed her back so she was forced to look at him, her face just inches from his.

"But I'll never get bored of being with you. Of listening to you. Even arguing with you turns me on. I take a perverse delight in getting you all riled up, just so I can see the fire in your eyes."

The magnetic pull of his voice, low and seductive, sent a frisson of electricity down Madeleine's spine. She forced herself not to get distracted by his soft lips, so close to hers. A long, deep sigh escaped from her.

"I realised I needed to trust you enough to know your own emotions. And if I didn't think mine would waver, then why should I think yours would?"

His hand came up and touched her cheek, brushing away another tear that fell. Madeleine drove herself to continue and not to give in to temptation and bury herself in his arms. She owed him an explanation for her behaviour.

"I was going to call you yesterday, but then the text from my mother, which obviously wasn't, had me running off in the wrong direction. I wanted to tell you how I felt face to face and instead dropped everything to save my mother." Her lips pulled down in a frown. "Exactly the kind of thing I accused you of with Chantal."

"It's not important, Madeleine."

Guilt itched at her conscience. She'd said so many awful things before. "I know that you will always do whatever you can for the people you love. I understand. I don't ever expect to come first."

"But you always will." His deep voice was steady.

"I don't expect you to come running to my side every time I get something wrong."

"But I always will." His tone held a note of patience, as if speaking to a small child that didn't fully grasp the situation. "Madeleine, when we are old and grey, I will still be there for you. Since you came into my life, the darkness has lifted. When you left, the shadows didn't return. Instead a new set of demons came to haunt me. What if you didn't come back into my life? What if you'd gone back to London and forgotten all about me? How would I survive knowing I'd had perfection within my grasp and I'd let it go because I wanted you to be the one to come to me?"

Her brow furrowed with a question, and he shrugged. "I told myself I'd give you a week to see reason." He breathed out a deep, resigned sigh. "In truth, I hardly lasted a few days. I was already planning to come and beg you to return when you called me."

He reached up and pulled her head down to his. Her heart stopped as she gazed into his dark eyes.

"I love you, Jean-Luc."

"And I love you, ma petite naïade."

He lifted his head and took her lips in his. The kiss started slowly, like a dance between two partners unsure of each other's next move, and then became urgent, more insistent. Her mouth opened to his, and he gripped the back of her neck, pulling her back down to the pillow with a groan. Her breasts grew heavy, and her nipples tightened in response to his tongue that dipped and stroked with hers. The warm taste of him filled Madeleine's senses, sending a heated rush between her thighs. She'd fantasized about this moment since she'd returned to her flat five days ago, but nothing compared to the real thing.

The alarm of the heart rate monitor started again. Madeleine pulled away from Jean-Luc, reluctant to bring their searing kiss to a close. When no one ventured into the room, she reached up and hit the reset button the nurse had pressed earlier.

"We're going back home tonight." His husky voice sent a glow of pleasure through her.

"I don't think they're going to allow that, Jean-Luc. You've been in and out of consciousness for the last few hours."

She smoothed his hair off his forehead. His hand covered hers, stilling her fingers. Her gaze flickered to his, and raw desire stared back at her.

"I don't give a damn about the doctors. After that kiss, all I want is you back in my bed where you belong."

She arched an eyebrow.

He grinned back at her. "I said I promised to put you first."

Laughter bubbled up inside her and spilled out. "You are the most impossible man."

Her phone beeped. She walked over to where she'd left it on the visitor's chair and picked it up.

"It's a message from Mum. She really is feeling terribly

guilty about what happened." She put the phone down without responding. At his questioning gaze, she shrugged. "I guess it won't harm her to stew in her own juices for once."

"I still don't understand how you thought Jackson was your mother."

She poured herself a glass of water from the jug beside his bed and took a sip. "I'm not sure I do, either. Jackson said it was spoofing, like people do with an email address. The police confirmed it. They said it came from a website people use to prank their friends."

"I presume he didn't get away?"

"No…" She wavered and warmth heated her cheeks. "I don't know how far he got." She straightened his bed covers for something to do. Her fingers moved over the sheet nervously. Jean-Luc kept silent, waiting for her to continue. The pressure to confess was almost as infuriating as the embarrassment. She groaned. "I fainted when you went under the water."

She lifted her head. His eyes glinted with teasing amusement.

"Ah, chérie, I do not deserve your devotion."

She glared daggers at him.

"Merde." He stifled back laughter. "I'm not strong enough for a fight."

"I've never fainted in my life." She cringed thinking about it. "And if you carry on smirking like that, I'll call the nurse back in and then we'll see about some pay-back."

He caught her hand and drew it across his chest, releasing it when she sat back down on the bed.

"Forgive me, chérie. The only one who deserves to pay

for his crimes is Jackson." His expression turned serious again. "Will your mother get her money back?"

"I suppose it will depend how much they find and how many others are demanding their share back, too."

His heartbeat was steady underneath her palm. The regular beat calmed her.

"Whatever happens, at least he won't be able to do it again. Well, not for a few years, anyway." He laid his hand over hers and closed his eyes. His thumb caressed her skin, and she felt his heart rate start to rise. Her own sped up in response. "The question still remains, what should be your punishment for stealing something that didn't belong to you?" A shiver of arousal went down Madeleine's spine at his seductive tone. His soft French accent washed over her, dragging her deeper into desire. "I've decided that I don't want my heart back. It's yours to keep."

Excitement sparked a reaction deep down inside her. "Thank you." Her voice was barely a whisper.

"I have decided on a fitting form of compensation, though."

Her lips tilted upwards into a smile. So had she, but they absolutely needed to be out of the hospital. "Oh. And what might that be?"

Jean-Luc opened his eyes and angled his head towards her. His gaze, as dark as night, held a hopeful expression. "Marry me."

"What?" She snatched her hand away from his. "You can't be serious." She stood and paced nervously across the room, peering again through the internal window. The nurses were still chatting at their station.

"Why not?" His voice sounded strained.

She turned around. Jean-Luc was staring at the ceiling. "We've only just met."

His gaze swivelled towards her. "So? I've rescued you twice now." He placed his hand across his chest. "I deserve the hand of the fair maiden."

"I'm not fair." She lifted a strand of hair to make the point.

"No, you're not, you're refusing to marry me." His expression was deadpan, but his eyes held a glint of determination.

A jolt of realisation hit her. She stood stock still in the middle of the room and smiled. A look of confusion came over Jean-Luc's face.

"You know what?" Madeleine held up her hands. "I'm waiting for the reaction to come. When you rescued me on the road, I remembered thinking I was just like my mother, falling for the first guy who came along. It annoyed me, infuriated me, and scared the hell out of me that I might become like her."

"And now?"

"I don't care. I think I like being rescued after all." Her smile widened. The joy came from deep within her, made her chest feel like bursting, and brought tears of happiness to her eyes.

"Good." Jean-Luc sounded smug.

"Why?"

"Because when I do it a third time, you're definitely marrying me. I demand compensation for how you've treated me. Taking advantage of my good nature."

"How I've treated you!" She stalked back around the bed. "I'm the one you were making wait a week. Not to mention that if anyone was taken advantage of the night Chantal screamed the place down, it was me."

His eyes stared back at her with a heated passion as they both remembered the night. He grabbed her hand and pulled her back onto the bed once more.

"Madeleine, shut up and kiss me."

She couldn't resist obeying his husky voice.

As their lips intertwined, he moved just a breath away. "I've been so lost without you, chérie. Say you'll stay this time."

"Always."

EPILOGUE

The golden rays of the setting sun streamed across the terrace. Their rich hues coloured everything from the grey stone of the chateau to the champagne glasses waiting to be filled.

A muscular arm slid around her waist and Madeleine leant back into Jean-Luc's embrace. Her breath caught as he placed a kiss on her neck. She turned her head and gazed up at him. "It's perfect."

"It is now you're here, my petite naïade."

His deep voice sent a thrill through her, and she wished they weren't waiting for guests to arrive.

Her gaze drifted to the beautiful diamond ring on her left hand and she sighed softly. "I still can't believe you carried this around until I said yes."

She felt Jean-Luc's lips raise into a smile against the top of her head. "I almost lost it twice."

Madeleine gasped and sped around to face him. "No! How?"

"One time I spilt something on my jacket. In my haste to

change, I forgot all about it. Fortunately, Danielle retrieved it before she sent the suit to the cleaners."

"And the other?"

He hesitated momentarily. "Much to my chagrin, coming back through customs after the fiasco with your mother. I should have declared it on the way out."

A flicker of ire shot through Madeleine. "If my mother had been responsible for losing my engagement ring before I'd even seen it, let alone wear it, I swear I'd never speak to her again."

Jean-Luc kissed her, drawing her lower lip sensually against his. Just as she was about to fall into his embrace, he pulled back a fraction. "On the other hand, we do have her to thank that you finally said yes."

Madeleine glared at him.

Jean-Luc's gaze darkened. "Don't look at me like that. You know I can't resist you when you're annoyed."

He leant down and kissed her again. This time, he pulled her tight against him, the hard proof of his arousal evident against her. It didn't matter that they only made love an hour before. One spark was all it took to rekindle the heat low within her.

She'd stopped worrying a long time ago that Jean-Luc could destroy her reasoned arguments if she let his lips do more than talk. Instead, she gave herself up to his seductive kiss and wrapped her arms around his neck.

Just as their passion ignited, Jean-Luc released her with a reluctant groan. "Chantal said she'd be down in a minute."

She gave him a wry smile. "Not to mention guests arriving and the wait staff about to run from the terrace in embarrassment."

"I don't know what comes over me every time you're near." His husky voice was thick with hunger.

Madeleine winked at him. "I've a pretty good idea."

A movement behind him caught her attention. She stood on tiptoe to look over Jean-Luc's shoulder. "Raph! You're early."

Dark eyes gazed back sheepishly at her. "Sorry."

She walked over hoping furiously that he hadn't been there long and greeted him with a kiss on both cheeks. "Don't be. It gives us a chance to have a few quiet words before everyone else arrives."

Jean-Luc followed her, detouring to pick up three glasses of champagne on the way. "I'm still not sure how I got talked into holding it here."

Madeleine dug him in the ribs with her elbow and turned to Raphael. "Take no notice of him. Chantal conned him into using the chateau for the soirée and he's been moaning ever since."

She took a sip of the champagne Jean-Luc passed her as Raphael gazed around him, taking in the transformation of the normally formal paved terrace to a romantic setting perfect for their engagement party.

"Chantal did this?"

Madeleine nodded, and Raph let out a low whistle of appreciation.

"It is beautiful, isn't it? She really loves that job in Paris. She was out here earlier, taking pictures for her portfolio. Wait until you see it at dusk." Madeleine smiled to herself, remembering last night when Chantal couldn't wait to show her and Jean-Luc how it would look once darkness came and hundreds of tiny fairy lights gave it an even more magical atmosphere.

"She's been dying to decorate out here for years." Raph turned towards Jean-Luc. "Do you remember those sketches she used to show us? Nothing quite like this, though."

"Don't let her hear you. She already has grand plans for the wedding."

Raphael raised his glass. "So, felicitations, at last." He leant over towards Madeleine. "How did he get you to commit?"

She turned to Jean-Luc and saw the amusement in his gaze. Madeleine's delaying tactics had become a standing joke. But it wasn't the back and forth to London for work, or any doubt on her part about Jean-Luc's love for her, which finally pushed her into agreeing.

The truth was simply that she couldn't bear to be parted from Jean-Luc any more than necessary. Plus, they wanted to start a family. No way was she going to leave their children to a series of nannies or cart them off to boarding school at the earliest chance.

Over the last few months, Jean-Luc had helped her start up a private consulting firm, which meant she could work from anywhere with just the occasional overnight stay.

Jean-Luc interrupted her thoughts. "We ended up rescuing her mother from some Arabian Prince intent on securing her for his harem. I was worried Madeleine might be next if she went alone."

Raph's lips rose a little and Jean-Luc reached out, drawing Madeleine close to him. The gentle squeeze around her waist reassured her that he was teasing.

Madeleine smiled, remembering the ludicrousness of the situation. "He exaggerates. It would never have got that far. Mum would have exhausted his highness long before any wedding took place."

Raph raised a brow and Madeleine lifted her gaze skywards.

"Not like that. Eww. I meant with her incessant demands."

Raph chuckled in response.

Madeleine pursed her lips. "I'm not making this any better, am I? Anyway, you can ask her all about it yourself this evening."

"But no police or thugs this time."

"No. All very civilized," interjected Jean-Luc.

Raph took a sip of his champagne. "I still can't believe it was a year since all that trouble in Nice."

"Talking of trouble. Did you say you were on your way to meet with Etienne?"

"Yes, he's hosting a private auction on the Spanish border. I said I'd meet him there."

Jean-Luc frowned. "I heard about that. I didn't imagine you'd be interested in a piece of jewellery, let alone something that will undoubtedly have dubious providence knowing him."

"I'm not. It just happens to be the most convenient time. He wants my advice on a property he's looking to buy, which is laughable considering the pair of us have been fighting over one property for years." Raph drained the last of his champagne. "Plus there's a woman."

"There always is," Jean-Luc remarked dryly.

Raph's lips twisted in a self-deprecating smile. "Well, wish me luck. I'm about to propose."

"You don't seem over-enthralled with the idea," said Madeleine.

"I'm not. Nor do I intend to marry her." Raph rubbed his temple with the palm of his hand. "I'm expected to produce a fiancée to secure a deal. I figured Caroline might be willing to pose as the future Madame Dauphin."

Madeleine frowned. "Are you going to give her some warning?"

Raph shook his head. "I figured it might be better to explain face to face."

Madeleine smirked. It was useless trying to talk some sense into him. He was just as stubborn as Jean-Luc once his mind was made up. "Don't be surprised if she shuts the door in your face."

"I hope not, because otherwise I'll need to find someone else, and fast."

He turned at the sound of footsteps from behind. Chantal's mocking, strident tone cut across the terrace. "Raphael, you've never been short of a woman prepared to do outrageous things for you in your life. I'm sure you'll think of something."

Raph leant down and greeted her with a kiss on both cheeks. "Salut, ma petite puce. The terrace looks amazing."

Chantal grimaced at the flea nickname, but her cheeks coloured and Madeleine could tell she was immensely pleased with the compliment. "Now, if you'll just excuse us a moment, I have a couple of last-minute discussions to have with Madeleine."

Chantal pulled her to one side. "Mon Dieu, if they are about to discuss property, you need rescuing from boredom. Allez. I feel the need to get your glass replenished and mine filled."

With a side trip to the server, Chantal tugged Madeleine over to the other side of the terrace to stare out over the river. Away from Jean-Luc and Raph, Madeleine gave in to her curiosity.

"Jean-Luc says Raph is always chasing someone."

"He is. But only because his heart was broken years ago." Chantal looked down at her glass. Her expression grew serious, while her gaze became reflective.

Madeleine nudged her. "Come on, what gives? If we're going to be sisters, you've got to tell me."

The left side of Chantal's mouth flicked up a little. "Don't think that I don't realise you're manipulating me with that sister act." She paused and then sighed. "I've no idea what happened, but I do know that it was when Jean-Luc was in England with Raph, while I was in the private hospital."

That explained her sudden change in temperament.

"She never returned his calls. I was too young to remember, but from what I've gleaned over the years, Raph brooded for a long while before going through a seemingly large number of women." She raised her eyebrows a little, and her eyes sparkled as if she'd stumbled upon a secret. "Maybe it was to blot one out?"

"The Caroline he's going to ask to marry him?"

Chantal tilted her head and scrunched up her nose. "No. I don't know who she is. Her name was Eva, or something similar. She was British, like you." She placed a hand on Madeleine's arm. "Perhaps you know her?"

Madeleine's face split into a grin at the absurdity of the question. "Like, oh you live in Paris, you must know my friend Marie."

Chantal laughed. "Okay, I take your point. I meant more that you move in the same circles. I seem to recall Jean-Luc saying that her family was very wealthy."

"Sorry. Never heard of her."

"Alors." Chantal dismissed their conversation with a flick of her wrist and lifted her champagne glass. "Enough about unrequited love. Let's toast to my soon-to-be-sister-in-law."

Several hours later, with the last of the guests finally gone, Madeleine leant over the balcony of the terrace and gazed into the distance.

The river rippled in the moonlight as it wound down the valley. The air was heavy with the scent of lavender and the sound of crickets chirping, interrupted only by the occasional rustling of something in the undergrowth beneath the terrace.

"What are you thinking so hard about?"

She turned and smiled at Jean-Luc. "You. Us. This." She raised a hand to encompass the chateau. "That night when you said you hoped there would be many more good memories to come. I think tonight counts."

He stepped closer and reached out, brushing a lock of hair back behind her ear. Cupping her cheek, he pulled her close and softly kissed her lips. "Tonight definitely counts. And the next night, and the next. So long as you're here. They're all good."

She kissed him back. "I think you might be a little delusional, but I like the sentiment."

"The only thing I'm crazy about is you."

Her heart skipped a beat and as his lips hit hers, Madeleine succumbed to the maelstrom of desire that burned within her.

Evie closed the door quietly behind her. She paused for a moment to scan the bedroom. It was neat and tidy. Not like some of the other rooms she'd attended to over the last couple of days.

But she couldn't complain. It was the perfect disguise. As one of the housekeeping staff for the private auction, her pass key gave her access to almost anywhere in the villa. With the right prop of a drink or pile of fresh towels, no one questioned her motives. Guests ignored her. Security just thought she was doing her job.

The only person she needed to avoid was Etienne. Which was why she needed to locate the safe and get out of his bedroom as quickly as possible. Although she'd taken steps to alter her appearance, there was no guarantee he wouldn't recognise her if they came face to face.

Did she still look the same as she did ten years ago? So much had happened since that time. So much lost. A fleeting thought of Raph popped into her mind, but she crushed it before sorrow pierced her heart.

Evie walked across the room and into the dressing area. The safe was exactly where she expected it to be, hidden behind a mirror. Her heart hammered in her chest, and she breathed deeply to fight down the wave of nausea that threatened to engulf her.

The longing to hold her necklace once more had driven her this far. She only needed to keep her nerve a little longer.

Willing her hand to remain steady, Evie entered the code her brother had given her and sent up a silent prayer to the gods of justice that it would work.

As she pressed the last digit, the sound of the lock unbolting sent a shiver of anticipation through her at the thought of claiming the pendant once more. While a rock landed in the pit of her stomach at just how loudly the click reverberated.

Convinced that someone must have heard the noise and

would come at any moment to investigate its cause, Evie jerked the door wide open.

Ignoring the cash, assorted papers, and passports, she reached for the velvet pouch. Tears of frustration, joy, and heartache welled up inside of her, but she forced them back. There was no time for emotion now.

She pulled aside the strings and tipped the contents into her hand. A large central ruby surrounded by emeralds and pearls winked back at her. She closed her eyes for a fraction of a second and clasped the necklace tight in her palm. An image flashed into her mind. Her grandmother, sitting in her favourite chair, a gentle smile on her lips as if to say Evie had done the right thing.

Footsteps out in the hallway reminded her how little time she had. Hastily, she slid the jewellery back into the pouch and eased it into her bag, double checking at the same time that her passport and purse were still in there.

She needed to leave the villa now. The more time she had before Etienne discovered it was missing, the further she could get away.

Opening the door to the hallway, Evie left the bedroom as silently as she'd come.

The Tangled Hearts series continues with Raphael and Evie's story in …
STEALING HEARTS

Stealing back her necklace was easy.

Keeping it is an entirely different problem.

Evie Madison's life changed irrevocably the night her grandmother's ruby pendant was brutally taken. Ten years later, the chance to steal it back is too good to resist.

But is it coincidence, or something more sinister, that the first person she meets is hardened property magnate, Raphael Dauphin—the man who broke her heart that same night a decade ago?

When fate places the woman he once loved back in his arms, Raph doesn't hesitate to take advantage. As security guards searching for Evie close in, he offers her a lifeline.

His protection, in exchange for posing as his fiancée to clinch a deal that's heading south.

Caught between the devil and the deep blue sea, the decision seems simple enough… but as the fire between Evie and Raph reignites, the dangers lurking in the shadows of the past awaken.

Suddenly it's not just her heart Evie's risking, but her life too.

Set in the glamorous South of France, STEALING HEARTS is a standalone, suspenseful romance featuring a sinfully sexy hero, a fake fiancée, and a genuine HEA.

"Adventure. Drama. Romance. Second chance romance done right... It was complex, smart, and still sexy." ★★★★★ — Lucretia, Goodreads

"A spellbinding book that keeps you on the edge of your seat throughout." ★★★★★ — Amazon Review

ABOUT THE AUTHOR

Sara Claridge writes contemporary romantic suspense. Born in West London, she inexplicably moved to France several years ago on a whim.

When not writing at her desk in the eaves of an old farmhouse, she can be found in the garden. Usually with a glass of red wine in one hand and a good book in the other.

www.saraclaridge.com

9 782957 078547